JORDAN'S GIFT

MIMI FOSTER

DEDICATION

For my niece, *Amanda Henry Sellet*,

author, encourager, hand holder when I didn't know what
I was doing. Thank you for your gift of helping me define
what was important and what to leave by the wayside. I
love you and wish great things for you.

This series contains adult content and is intended for mature readers. Each of the five books in the Thunder on the Mountain series is a complete, stand-alone story.

Thunder Snow (Contemporary – Book 1)
Thunder Struck (Contemporary – Book 2)
Thunder Storm (Contemporary – Book 3)
Jordan's Gift (Historical – Book 4)
Willow's Secret (Historical – Book 5)

In *Thunder Struck*, Jordan and Brandan discover century-old journals. I was so enamored with the people who wrote the journals (the original Jordan and her daughter Willow), I decided to write their stories. Preferring conflict to come from external sources rather than the relationship, this series is fun, tender, and deliciously steamy.

PRAISE FOR MIMI FOSTER

Absolutely my favorite

This is the best book I've ever read. I couldn't put it down! Loved the mystery surrounding Jack. He was a genuine romantic and from the beginning Callie fell in love with his rather rough exterior. They are the perfect couple.

Mary Rath on THUNDER SNOW

Absolutely and utterly Brilliant!! MUST READ!!!

I cannot even begin to tell you how much I LOVED this book!! Every single moment and every single page was like Christmas morning. Jordan and Brandan are two of the most beautifully developed and wonderfully written characters. Ms. Foster, you are now on my MUST READ ANYTHING YOU WRITE list!!

Amazeballs Book Addicts on THUNDER STRUCK

It just gets better and better

This series is positively addictive. It's kind of like giving heroine to an addict. Once you start the stories in this series you just can't put them down.

Joyce Ruskuski on THUNDER STORM

Truly a Gift

Mimi Foster continues to capture my imagination with warm and sensual characters, enchanting settings, and beautiful romance. Jordan and Edward are magnetic, and the non-stop fire between them kept me sizzling page after page!

P. Stachel on JORDAN'S GIFT

Best. Book. Ever.

A beautiful story that captured life and captured me. Foster captured how many of us are when we are alone, when no one is looking. When we don't like what or who we see when we look in the mirror but someone else can see our beauty. This is absolutely one of the best books ever.

Anne Marie Smith on MAISY'S MIRROR

JORDAN'S GIFT
Copyright © 2014 by Mimi Foster

ISBN: 9780986291203
ASIN: B00Q23M19W

Cover design by The Killion Group
http://thekilliongroupinc.com

Chapter One

THE MEETING

*H*e didn't consider himself hard-hearted, he just hated people. Stupid ones were everywhere.

He was itching for a fight as he headed to town to pick up supplies. He didn't recognize the dark gold Palomino carrying hand-tooled saddlebags waiting patiently outside the General Store. First person to cross him was going to be sorry they'd gotten in his way, and a stranger would suit him just fine. Luck was on someone's side when he saw he was the only patron in the store, but he could hear Dorothy's raised voice in the back room.

"You need to listen to reason, Jordan."

"I'm not going back. Nothing anyone can say or do will induce me to go through with the wedding."

"Maybe there's a simple explanation for what you saw."

"If you don't want me to stay with you, I'll make other arrangements, Aunt Dorothy. This seemed like a good place to hide until the gossip dies down, and I thought I could help you."

Edward didn't want to eavesdrop and he certainly didn't care about the broken heart of young girl, but her voice was pleading and he was interested to see how his friend Dorothy would respond to the desperation in her argument.

"Of course you can stay, but you're making a big mistake. Men have affairs all the time, and you could do a lot worse than Andrew Harriman."

The hair on the back of his neck stood up at the mention of the name. He and Andrew had been opponents for at least a decade. He despised everything about his rival, and questioned what illicit thing he was involved with now.

"Call me crazy, but I expect to marry a man who takes his vows seriously. Life's hard enough to not have to worry about infidelity. I'll die an old maid rather than chain myself to a two-timing louse."

Edward thought her description not only appropriate, but felt the young woman had a narrow escape by not being shackled to such a disreputable man.

"Being away will give you time to reconsider."

"Being away will give him time to forget my existence. He tried every excuse he could think of, but I'm done. Please, it's not an option and never will be. Can we leave it at that?"

"I'm not sure Nederland is the right place for a rich, attractive young woman, but you're welcome to stay, you know that. Lord knows I can use the help."

"Oh, thank you! I promise you won't be sorry. It'll be just like old times."

"It's long days of hard work. You head on up to the house and get your things unpacked. You can have your old room. I'll see you in a while."

He started to turn away so as not to appear to have been listening, but when the magnificent creature with dark auburn hair and flawless features stepped through the curtain, he didn't think he could have moved if his life depended on it. She was strikingly feminine, and he was conscious he'd stopped breathing when their gazes met. Her blue eyes were like a sapphire he'd once seen, but he couldn't remember where. Hell, he couldn't even remember where he was.

"Edward, good to see you. You haven't been around in a while." Dorothy said, following her niece out of the office.

He knew he had to respond, knew he had to move from his frozen position, knew he had to take his eyes off the young lady who stood so poised in front of him. "Afternoon, Dorothy," he said finally, breaking whatever spell the youthful enchantress had cast. "Running out of a few basics and thought I'd stock up before heading up the pass." He wondered if he was breathing normally yet; wondered if Dorothy would notice anything different; wondered what in the world had made him stupid.

"You know where everything is. Give a shout if I can help," she said. "Oh, this is my niece, Jordan Calhoun. She's going to be helping me for a while. Jordan, Edward Stratton."

After a brief pause, Jordan's delicate tongue licked her

lower lip and the husky timbre of her voice could be felt to his toes. "How do you do, Mr. Stratton?" He knew he appeared rude but didn't particularly care. A nod was all he could muster as he turned to examine a pair of chaps hanging on the wall because he couldn't think of anything to say. He'd never reacted like that to another human in his life, and he was sure he didn't like it.

"SO TELL ME ABOUT EDWARD STRATTON," JORDAN ASKED her aunt that evening as they ate the meal she'd prepared while Dorothy was at work. Tomorrow would be soon enough for Jordan to start at the store, but today she'd spent the afternoon cleaning house. It was obvious there wasn't a lot of time to do simple chores around here, and Jordan wanted to be helpful.

"Tough as nails, doesn't take nonsense from anyone, and people wear him down asking for jobs, handouts, you name it. Keeps to himself mostly. I imagine it would be rough owning the tungsten mines and knowing any one of the drifters who come through town would kill you just as soon as look at you to get what you've worked so hard for."

"He owns the mines?" Jordan asked, remembering the man who had rendered her nearly speechless earlier in the day. He had to have been well over six feet, eyes the color of coal, and she had the strangest notion when she was captured by his gaze that the color reflected his soul.

"He's the biggest employer in the area. Treats his men fairly, pays a fair wage for a day's work, doesn't have time for cheats or fighting. Runs a tight ship, but his men would die for him, and he makes sure they're well taken care of. He comes into town every week or so, but he's not a man I'd want to cross."

"Is he married?"

Her aunt looked at her with surprise. "Don't go getting any notions about Edward Stratton. Handsome as sin, but I've known him for years and I've never seen him even glance at a woman. But that doesn't stop them from trying. Trust me, the ones around here go out of their way to get his attention. Make fools of themselves, they do. Like I said, keeps to himself, doesn't let anyone get close."

"I was just asking. He seemed interesting."

"Yeah, interesting like a shark in rough waters. He's a deep one."

She'd been engaged to Andrew for five weeks and had a hard time remembering what he looked like. She'd been in Edward's presence less than five minutes and couldn't think of anything else but their encounter. His face was the last thing she saw as she fell asleep that night.

FOR THE THIRD TIME THIS MONTH HE STOOD ON THE SIDE of the mountain at the entrance to the mine and stopped a railcar from leaving on the long journey to have its cargo weighed and processed. Edward looked at the overseer, a normally competent man who had a puzzled look as he pulled at his long beard with one hand and held onto a suspender with the other. Edward was at a loss to explain why they suddenly didn't understand how much time and money was lost if a wooden ore-cart left at half capacity. Were they being deliberately obtuse?

He looked at a surrounding group of miners who were leaning against their pick axes and shovels, listening to the encounter. There were a dozen dirty men with kerchiefs around their necks, many who had worked for him for years. "Every one of you understands the situation here," Edward said, looking from one to another and receiving a nod from all.

He turned to the foreman. "There are enough good men looking for work, Angus. I'll have no problem firing you if it happens again. Are we clear?"

"Yes, Mr. Stratton," he said, still with a perplexed look.

For the third time that month he was assured it wouldn't happen again. He knew Angus to be a good leader and a good man. When there weren't so many around, he'd speak with him privately. There had to be another explanation.

Or was he getting soft? He should have fired him on the spot.

She'd put in a long day at the store and was exhausted. "I'll head up to the house and get dinner ready," she called to her aunt. "Try not to be too much longer."

She looked up when the bell jingled and froze as she was hanging her apron behind the counter. "Jordan, can you take care of whoever it is, please?" Dorothy asked in a loud whisper. "I'm up to my elbows in flour."

It took a minute to realize she'd been spoken to. "Of

course," she said, surprised how husky her voice sounded. "I'm in no hurry." She was captured in his stare. He'd taken off his hat and his long hair was a creamy, rich chocolate brown with waves that framed his face. His eyes were dark as obsidian, and she felt herself falling into his depths, unable to break their contact. She didn't mind how long they stood there. He had an intriguing combination of features, and she was content to study his rugged chin, the elegant length of his nose, and lips that held a strange fascination for her, even though they hadn't moved in the slightest since she'd been looking at them.

He didn't seem to be in any more of a hurry than she, and she wasn't anxious to break the spell. The peculiar things going on in her chest were curious, and she examined her reaction while she studied the extraordinary man before her. It took supreme concentration for her to finally ask, "Is there something in particular you're looking for?"

He broke their trance and looked at the shelf behind her. "Coffee," he finally said in a voice she was sure could melt the butter in the churn.

You can do this, Jordan, she thought. *One foot in front of the other, get the burlap, get the scoop, measure, weigh. You've done this half a dozen times today. You just have to move.*

"How much would you like?" Was that her voice?

"All of it."

"You want *all* the coffee?" she asked, trying to understand what he'd said.

"The what?" He seemed to come out of whatever fog he'd been in and said, "No, just a pound." He turned away and looked at the same pair of chaps he'd examined so closely the day before. What on earth was the matter with him?

"I have your coffee ready." She stood at the cash register, not bothering to play coy, appreciating what she saw.

He stepped forward and was proud of himself for being able to go through the motion of pulling out his money packet. He gave her the twenty cents, but when his hand touched hers, they both felt the shock of contact. Their eyes shot to each other. He pulled back like he'd been burned with a poker, picked up his coffee, and walked out the door without a word.

He felt all kinds of a fool as he rode out of town like the hounds of hell were attacking. He hadn't been able to get her out of his mind all day. He'd been sure if he saw her again, he'd realize there wasn't a need for her invading his thoughts like a conquering army. Instead, he'd seen her standing there, saw her arms raised and the material of her dress straining against her well-defined figure, saw the blue of her eyes as they locked with his, and he surrendered, knowing he'd never be the same.

He'd spent most of his life frozen inside, in the company of rough and dangerous men. He was bitter and cynical to his core, and in two encounters that had lasted less than ten minutes, a young slip of a girl with a captivating smile, luxuriant brownish-red hair, clear eyes as blue as a lake at high noon had turned him inside out and made him a stuttering simpleton. Did she think him deaf and dumb from the vacant look he constantly wore?

Jordan could think of nothing but the feeling that shot through her at his touch, and was curious if he'd reacted the same way. She'd had men court her for years, had even agreed to marry Andrew, but none of them made her heart dissolve to her toes, or made her breath quicken, or made her anxious to see them. Dorothy said he stopped in every week or so. She wasn't sure she'd hold up waiting that long for his next visit.

SHE HADN'T HEARD THE BELL AS SHE WAS GETTING READY TO leave the next day, but she knew he was there by the strange flutter and expansion in her heart. When she turned and saw him, her lips smiled in welcome.

Dorothy said, "Well, good afternoon, Edward," having no clue her niece drew him like a full moon drew the tide. He speculated whether or not the electricity shooting between them would singe her aunt, because he was now convinced Jordan was having the same reaction. "Good to see you again. What can we get for you?" she asked, interrupting his thoughts.

"Bacon." He said the first thing that came to mind, his eyes never leaving Jordan's.

"Jordan can ring you up while I cut off a slab. How much do you want?" she asked as she headed behind the curtain.

His lips moved in an upward curve as he remembered the response he'd given Jordan the day before. "A pound will do today."

When he smiled, Jordan felt as though the sun had come from behind a cloud. Her heartbeat was a fluttering thrum. It was bewitching, and the air seemed suddenly to be filled with color. "That will be twenty eight cents, Mr. Stratton."

"Call me Edward." Her eyes flew to his.

"Yes, sir. That will be twenty eight cents, please."

"Call me Edward."

"All right, Edward, how about you hand over your money and no one gets hurt?"

His booming laughter could be felt along her nerve endings. He'd wanted to hear his name on her lips but hadn't expected her sass.

THE PROPOSAL

"**I**'ve known Edward for at least six years," Dorothy commented when he'd paid and left. "That's the first time I've heard him laugh." She looked questioningly at her niece. Not wanting to engage, Jordan put on her sweater and walked up the hill with a smile that glowed like the setting sun. It had been a good day.

The routine continued for weeks, Edward asking for one item, a few words being exchanged, then leaving. She looked forward to the thunder of her pulse when he stepped through the door, and her days went faster with a sense of heady anticipation of his daily arrival.

When he didn't show up one afternoon, she was dejected. She found things to do for an extra half hour, but knew dinner wouldn't be ready in time if she waited any longer. She was surprised how lonely she felt in not having seen him that day. Was he tired of the game they played?

She crossed the street and turned toward home, her footsteps heavy as she made her way slower than she'd been all week, wondering if he'd been busy or purposely didn't come to see her. The quickening of her pulse alerted her to his presence.

"May I walk you home?" His voice was close, but didn't startle her because she already knew he was there.

"If you've nothing better to do with your time, be my guest."

At least a foot taller than she, he cast her a sideways glance, then laughed a rumbling sound that seemed to come from his soul.

"If you're inquiring if I'd rather oversee ore shipments, or break up fights between men who've been together too long, or explain to another clodpate the same lesson I've imparted numerous times before, *or* I'd rather walk a beautiful young lady to her door in the cool of twilight, I'll choose the latter. Thank you for asking."

They smiled at each other. Her spirit was lighter, but she didn't pick up her pace because she didn't want it to be over too soon.

"Are you enjoying your time in this God-forsaken place?" he asked good-humoredly.

"I love it here, actually. There's so much convention that needs to be adhered to in Denver, so many proprieties that need to be followed. I'm much more comfortable here. My aunt has called me a 'hoyden' on more than one occasion." She looked at him to judge his reaction.

"Nothing wrong with that," he said immediately. "No one's ever accused me of caring what others think."

"I can believe that," she said. "You seem to be a man who makes the rules rather than follow them."

He studied her for a moment. "Perceptive of you."

The shock of eye contact made her pulse quicken. "I feel like I've already been a big help to Dorothy." She tried to break the spell. "She has so much to do, and things had slipped through the cracks. Being here has given me a chance to get things in order for her at the house and the store, and I enjoy feeding her. I know gentle-bred ladies aren't supposed to know how to cook, but it's another unconventional thing I've enjoyed learning over the years."

"Certainly not a bad asset for anyone to possess."

"You from around here?" Why did she suddenly feel nervous?

"I've lived a lot of places, but I've been here long enough to think of it as 'home.'"

"Denver's home to me, but we traveled a lot. I spent enough time in Nederland to consider it a second home. I'd much rather be here."

"Strange I've never seen you around." Again they looked at each other, and her reaction had her trying to figure out how she'd take her next breath.

"I love walking in the meadow when I have free time," she said, changing the subject. "I have a special rock where I read when time permits."

They strolled in companionable silence for a few minutes. "I've never seen the meadow as anything but a plot of land to get across when traveling from one place to the next," he said. "I'll have a different appreciation for it now." His voice was mellow.

They were at her door in too short a time for her liking. "Thank you for the pleasant diversion, Miss Calhoun." She climbed the step to the front porch.

"Call me Jordan."

"You don't have to ask me twice," he teased. He leaned forward and touched her cheek because at that moment, the feel of her was the most important thing in his world. She closed her eyes, savoring the warmth of his touch.

He turned, breaking the spell. "I'll see you soon," he said over his shoulder, flipping his hat onto his head as he walked away whistling.

THE NEXT DAY HE DIDN'T SHOW UP AT THE STORE, BUT SHE didn't stay late waiting for him, hoping she'd see him on her way home. As she crossed the street, he was coming out of the building that was used as their post office, telegraph office, and bank. "Mind if I join you?"

"Is there a reason I should?"

After a moment he said, "If you could see my thoughts, it might give you pause."

His words made her hesitate. When her nerves began to settle, she resumed walking. "If you could see *my* thoughts, you'd know I don't mind at all." She knew her cheeks flamed with her bold words, but she was as interested as he appeared to be. She'd never been a wallflower and she had no intention of letting life pass her by.

He smiled. "You're like a breath of fresh air to a trapped miner."

"Distressing thought, but thank you, I think."

When they could see her house, his pace slowed. "I need to ask you something."

"I'm not much into secrets. Ask away."

"Are you still in love with him?"

"In love with whom?" she said, puzzled, coming to a standstill.

"The bells didn't alert you to my presence the first day, and I heard your discussion with Dorothy about your broken engagement."

She smiled and started walking again. "Oh, Andrew, I thought you meant someone important." She couldn't have said anything to set his mind more at ease. He didn't have to warn her then, she seemed intuitive enough to see him for what he was. More importantly, he wasn't going to have to fight him for her affections. "Fact of the matter is, I was never in love with him, never even remotely thought I was."

"Then why did you agree to marry him?"

"It's a little complicated, but I don't mind telling you if you're interested."

"You must know I am."

If she had known this feeling he caused existed, she would never have agreed to Andrew's proposal. "Do you have a few minutes? I could take you to my rock in the meadow."

"I'd be honored."

As they walked, she told him about her parents. "They're Denver socialites who like to travel. Dorothy is mother's sister. She met a man and fell in love, and they came to Nederland and opened the store. Dorothy hated city life, and when her husband died, she knew enough about the business and had the respect of the locals, so she decided to stay."

"Was your mother upset?"

"Very. She and their other sister, Phoebe, tried and tried to get her to come back, but she's happy here, and finally they stopped trying. I lived with Phoebe on and off all my life when my parents traveled. She taught me to quilt and play the piano, and I loved those times. But I also enjoyed the times I would stay with Dorothy and help out, especially as I got older."

They arrived at her rock in the meadow. Edward sat on the ground and leaned against it as she sat above him on the sun-warmed smoothness.

"Tell me about Andrew," he said quietly, his shoulder touching her leg. She was glad she couldn't see his face but found comfort in having him near.

"During the past eighteen months I've had a handful of marriage proposals. My father always said I could choose whom I would marry, and both of my parents wanted me to fall in love and be devoted to a spouse like they are to each other. But I feared after turning down several that I would never find what they were talking about."

"But you felt something for Andrew?"

"Good Lord, no. He was nice enough, charming to be sure. But he was a widower with a young son who needed a mother. Andrew and I got along peacefully, he appeared to be a good match, but Adler was five and he was the reason I finally agreed to marry Andrew. I've always wanted children, he seemed like a good start."

"What happened to change your mind?"

Remembering that day, she now felt relief and thankfulness it happened. "I'd picked up a small toy for Adler and was going to drop it off. As I came up the sidewalk I could see Andrew through the window in the parlor with a young woman. I hesitated, wondering who she was. When he embraced and kissed her passionately, I thought I must be mistaken."

They sat close to each other with a calm sense of an old friendship. "I'm sorry for the pain it caused, but I'm not sorry it happened," he said quietly.

"He had never attempted to kiss me in such a manner, and I stood watching, completely separated and unhurt by what I was seeing, but when his hand reached for her breast, I turned and hurried home, trying to decide what to do next."

"What *did* you do?"

"I had a note delivered to him, along with his engagement ring, and told him never to contact me again. I foolishly believed that would be the end of his involvement in my life."

"Go on," he said, sitting up, pulling a blade of grass.

"The first time he came by, he wanted an explanation. When I gave it to him, he was incredulous and told me I'd gotten it all wrong. The second time he tried to tell me it was his cousin and I was mistaken, that it was just a warm farewell to someone with whom he was close. The third time, he had Adler knock on my door and hand me a flower while he stood on the sidewalk."

"Swine," he said.

"You are correct. At first I hurt for the little boy, but when I looked up at Andrew and saw he thought he'd won, I hardened my heart and vowed not to deal with his lies. I packed my bags and came to visit Dorothy that very afternoon."

"And that was the day I met you."

"Yes. I figure after a short period of time, he'll move on to greener pastures and not look for me any more. I can stay with Dorothy as long as I want."

Edward stood and took her hand, helping her slide from the rock. As she gained her balance, he put his arms around her. Her face was pressed tightly against his chest. Their pulses seemed to be in harmony. She'd never felt like this, and she'd never known a man with whom she could share such intimate feelings. There was healing in his embrace.

He took her hand, kissed it, and continued to hold on to it as he walked her home. She felt protected. "Did you enjoy kissing Andrew?" he asked as they approached the house.

"You mean did something besides my gut pucker?" She may have shuddered. "Fact of the matter is, I felt nothing when kissing him except cold. I wanted so much to find the warmth, the desire." She looked away and knew her cheeks were flaming. "I wanted what I felt when I looked up and saw you standing in the store."

"Minx," he said, lifting her face toward his, yielding to the inevitable. "Let's see if we can help you find that spark."

Whatever he was expecting, it wasn't the explosion that tore through his body as their lips met. He pulled her as close as possible and teased her mouth open with his tongue. She held nothing back, dueling with him, giving as good as she got. He was hardness to her soft, and he didn't know how he was going to be able to stop. How could he possibly let her go after this? The palm of her hands ran up his muscular arms and she moaned. It was his undoing.

He pulled his mouth away but continued to hold her close, as though by that action he could stem the pounding beats of his heart. He was afraid he'd break her if he held her any tighter and eased his embrace. He could feel her shaking against him and feared she might be crying.

"What is it?" he asked, genuinely concerned as he lifted her chin to meet his gaze. Relief swept through him when he saw the smile on her face.

Her eyes were alight when she said, "Why didn't you tell me it could be like this?"

His answering grin told her he was pleased with her response. "I let you know as quickly as I possibly could," he teased. "Dorothy would have thought I'd lost my mind if I'd done what I wanted and thrown you over my shoulder and ridden off into the sunset."

"You'll have to do that sometime."

He was encouraged by what he'd heard. They stood on the porch, neither wanting their interlude to end. In a short period of time, she'd turned his life upside down. He said quietly, "My heart's been encased in ice for as long as I can remember. When our lips met, I could feel chunks of it breaking away. Call me fanciful, but it's like your heat was melting it."

When he saw her tears, he was concerned. "Have I hurt you?"

"Of course not. I'm just overwhelmed. Do you have to leave?"

"You need to get dinner going or Dorothy will wonder what you've been doing."

"I was doing the only thing I've wanted to do for the past four weeks," she said without reservation. "Will I see you tomorrow?"

"Can you imagine you wouldn't?"

"I can't imagine how people walk around feeling like this. Now I know what my parents were talking about."

A WEEK LATER THEY WERE SITTING ON HER ROCK, HER BACK against him, his arms around her waist, his chin leaning on her head. "Tell me about your childhood," she prompted softly.

"What do you want to know? There's not a lot to tell. I was shuffled from grandparents to aunts and uncles until I was old enough to run away and prospect."

"What happened to your parents?"

"My father left to find gold when I was three. Never came back. My mother died of consumption when I was eight."

Her heart broke for the little boy he'd been. "Do you remember much about her?"

"There are a few distinct memories, the most intense being she loved to ice skate. She had me skating almost from the time I could walk. Nothing specific, only there was a pond near our house and we'd spend hours there. She'd tell me it made her feel like she could fly."

Jordan took his hand and held it against her chest. "My favorite part was, when we got home she'd fix hot chocolate and tell me adventure tales, tales of King Arthur and Odysseus and Paul Bunyan and Hercules. I wanted to find one of them to make her better."

Jordan kissed his hand, wishing she could heal him.

"Nothing can be done to change what's past," he said. "We only have today, and I'm where I want to be."

IT WAS ANOTHER WEEK BEFORE THE TELEGRAM HE'D BEEN waiting for arrived. He'd tracked her parents down in Paris and sent the following message: *Your daughter is in love [stop] Says she's found what you've been talking about [stop] I can provide well for her [stop] Permission to marry [stop] ~ Edward A. Stratton*

He was not a man of convention but wanted to make sure everything he did was for Jordan, and that she would have no regrets. When the telegram finally came, it said simply: *Permission to marry granted [stop] ~ Carl and Cicely Calhoun*

He wasn't a patient man and the last week had been a strain, but he wanted to do this right. He couldn't wait until the end of the day. Dorothy was standing with an armload of boxes when he arrived at the store. Edward took them from her and placed them where she directed. "May I take Jordan away for a while?" he asked, anxious to get on with it. "I would like to abscond with her heart." A teasing smile played on his face.

Dorothy looked him in the eye and said, "You'd better not hurt her or you'll answer to me."

"You'll never need to be concerned about that," he said solemnly.

"Jordan!" she called, continuing to look at him. "Someone's here to see you."

Jordan came in from the back room, her laugh sudden and happy. The thrill of seeing Edward there was as exciting as it had been the first time. With a wicked grin, he removed her apron, nodded at Dorothy, then picked Jordan up and threw her over his shoulder. She was shocked, then laughter bubbled as she relaxed against his back. He was on his horse in one swift move, and slid her down facing him as he took off in a cantor.

She held on, head against his chest, not caring in the least where he was taking her as long as they were together. What could Dorothy possibly be thinking about this turn of events? As they arrived at her rock in the meadow, he put his foot in the stirrup and lifted her down gently with him. "I'm sorry I didn't take you off into the sunset, but I thought this would be more appropriate."

"It will never just be my spot again, it will always be our spot." Her look conveyed all the emotion flowing from her.

"The last time I remember feeling anything that resembled warm emotion was before my mother died," he said, patting the rock next to him, pulling her close so her head rested on his chest. "You changed all that. I want to spend the rest of my life providing for you and our children." He pulled the telegrams out of his pocket and handed them to her.

When she was done reading, she hopped down and

faced him, hands on his knees. "Is this a proposal of marriage?" she asked with a half grin.

"No, actually *this* is a proposal of marriage," he said, pulling an exquisite diamond ring out of its resting place in his other pocket. "Jordan Lillian Calhoun, will you do me the honor of being my wife?"

She threw herself into his arms, kissing him all over his face. "Yes, yes, yes! I thought you'd never ask," she said, laughing and crying at the same time. He slid the ring on her finger and everything he knew righted itself on its axis. She was going to marry him.

"I'm giving you the option," he said. "We can have a large society wedding in six weeks time when your parents return from their vacation, or we can be married in a small ceremony this weekend with a few people and celebrate with a grand party after your folks get back."

She tapped her finger on her lip as though seriously considering the possibilities. "Which would you prefer?"

"Oh, you know me. I definitely want to wait for your parents – wait all that time to bed you, wait all that time so we can be fodder for the society tabloids. That would suit me just fine."

They laughed just before their lips met. The heat that scorched them every time they came together ignited, and Jordan pulled away breathless. "There's not a part of me that doesn't want you," she said without embarrassment, trying to pull his tucked shirt out of its confinement as he groaned against her neck.

"Jordan, Jordan, don't do this, you have no idea how much I want you." He couldn't stop touching her. "The ride over here almost did me in."

"I've been yours since the day I first saw you standing in Dorothy's store."

He took hold of her hands with his much larger ones and wound them around his neck. He held her face and kissed her eyes and the tip of her nose. His tongue smoothed her lips until they were desperate for possession. "As much as I want to take you right here and now, I want you to be my wife in both name and fact."

"Is it horrible of me to not want to wait?"

"The first time I take you, you'll be Mrs. Edward A. Stratton. It's important that you're mine in every way. But I have no problem starting your education in the satisfaction to be found between a man and a woman," he said, taking her lips and showing her a taste of the lifetime they'd have of fulfillment.

Chapter Three

THE HOUSE

*I*t was Thursday and they were to be married two days hence on Saturday. Edward was alternately frustrated and proud that Jordan wouldn't leave Dorothy alone in the shop until the person Edward had hired to replace Jordan arrived, which should be early this afternoon. Even trying to reason with her that Dorothy had been running her business for years without any help would not sway his bride-to-be. He was leaning casually against the telegraph pole at the depot waiting for the coach when he looked down the street toward Dorothy's store and saw Jordan talking with someone.

Something about the way she was moving alarmed him, and he knew she was angry. When she moved slightly, he saw the tall blond man leaning over her. Rage made him see red. It couldn't have been more than thirty seconds, but it felt like it took forever to cross the street. When he came around the corner he saw Andrew grab her wrist as she raised her hand.

"You *will* come back with me," Andrew said in not-quite a shout. "You have made me a laughing stock and I demand you return at once and honor our engagement."

The sound of the hammer on Edward's gun echoed in the silence that followed. Andrew and Jordan turned as one to find Edward propped languidly against a porch post fondling his pistol, barrel pointed straight at Andrew's chest.

"Edward!" she said, rushing to his side, throwing her arms around his waist. As he settled his free arm around her, the overpowering peace of knowing she'd unconsciously chosen him without hesitation cracked whatever pieces of ice had remained encased around his heart. Her fate was irrevocably sealed with his from that moment forward.

"I believe you have your answer, Harriman. If you even so much as look like you're going to argue, I'll make your little boy an orphan before your next breath. Now get on your horse and ride out of town. Jordan is mine and I don't share – ever."

There was a charged pause as Jordan waited to see if Andrew would back down in this atmosphere saturated with disaster. She had no doubt Edward would follow through on his promise to put a bullet in him, and she was equally sure he'd take pleasure in doing so.

Andrew's gaze was cloaked in haughtiness as he looked from one to the other. After what seemed an eternity, he turned on his heel, untethered his horse, and left in a cloud of dust. Holstering his gun, Edward looked at the woman who remained attached to his side, unspoken words lying deep in his eyes. "Have I mentioned this morning how much I love you?" he asked conversationally.

She was laughing as she straightened and let go of his waist. "No, I don't believe you have." Making a play at smoothing her skirt, she said calmly, "I'm not sure I've ever been more glad to see anyone in my life." She rubbed her arms as if cold, then wrapped them around her stomach.

"What's the matter?" he asked, pulling her toward him.

"He scares me, Edward. You've not only humiliated him, you've thwarted him. I can't imagine that will bode well for us."

"He can't hurt us now, Jordan. You're mine, and nothing but death will ever take you from me. And as much as I'm sorry for the hurt he caused, I'll be forever grateful it happened. I found my life's breath the day I walked into Dorothy's store and saw you there."

THE WEDDING WAS HELD IN THE MEADOW BY THEIR ROCK. Only Dorothy and her new clerk were invited. Edward didn't want anyone intruding on this personal ceremony. There would be plenty of time for the world's interruption later. He wore Levi's and a starched white shirt; Jordan wore an exquisite lace dress that Edward had delivered the previous day on a coach from Denver. Dorothy's tears ran unheeded as she held Jordan's flowers and Edward kissed his bride.

Edward had plans for his young spouse, so there would be no gathering afterwards. Everyone had left and she was sitting in front of him, his arms holding her, riding gently out of the meadow. She raised a hand and touched his face that kept finding its way to the crook of her neck.

"May I ask the stupidest question ever asked by a bride?"

"There is nothing that would ever make me think you could utter something stupid. What's your question?"

"Where are we going to live?" She was quite serious.

The rumble started deep in his chest and the sound of his laughter brought her joy, and a flush to her cheeks. "I told you it was a stupid question. Until this moment it's never actually occurred to me to wonder."

The horse continued to walk slowly toward their destination, wherever that was. Edward squeezed her and ran his hand over her breast, feeling her harden under his palms. "Can you imagine what it does to me to know you love me for who I am and don't care where we live as long as we're together?"

"Most of that's the truth," she said, head bowed, almost like a confession. "Truth be told, I'd rather not live in a tent."

Again the deep response that so pleased her could be felt along her spine.

"Most strangers don't care who I am, but for whatever reason they feel I should be sharing my wealth with them. There have been days I've left the house through a secret exit, dressed as a pauper or a woman or a stooped old man with a beard."

She tried to turn in the saddle to see whether or not he told the truth. "I'm not jesting," he answered her unspoken question. "People everywhere want something for nothing. It's why I left Denver and moved here nearer the mines, so there weren't quite so many to fend off daily."

"Oh, Edward, I had no idea. That's terrible. I'm sorry."

"Nothing to be sorry about. I know whom I'll help and whom I won't. And if they ask for a handout, the answer's 'no.'"

"Then how do you know?"

"I've become good at being a silent, unnoticed observer of those who are truly in need. Then I find a way to make their lives easier. Great wealth bears great responsibility."

"What have I ever done in my life to deserve you?"

He kissed her head. "I, too, keep thinking you must be a dream. I'll do as much as I can to protect you, but I want nothing to do with most people. Your aunt was one of the few who was genuinely kind to me."

"And again, I will forever be grateful you hired help for her. Eugene is strong and intelligent, and Dorothy would never admit it, but she's getting too old to carry the boxes and heavy supplies necessary to run the store. To say nothing of the fact she works at least eleven-hour days. Having someone to help will give her time off. She might even be able to visit her sisters every now and then."

They left the meadow and traveled up the hillside to the north side of town. Small structures were scattered into the distance. Jordan had never been up here, and Edward stopped before they came over the rise. "What are those?"

"Wickiups. You see some are shaped like a traditional tipi, some are rounded? The frames are made from willow branches and then covered with hide or tree brush. The Utes help at the mine sometimes, but mostly they keep to themselves."

He got down and helped her maneuver in her lace gown. They walked slowly hand in hand.

"By the way, I had your horse and what few possessions you have with you brought to the house earlier. We'll go to Denver soon and retrieve your things, or go on a mad shopping spree, whichever you prefer," he said with a lopsided grin.

"There's not much I need. I am content . . . and ready to be your wife."

He held her, her cheek resting on his chest. "I want to explain something."

"Sounds serious. Is it going to make me run screaming into the night?"

She savored his warming laugh. She wanted to give him years of laughter. "Nothing so dramatic." He took her hand and continued walking.

"For reasons I could never explain, I hired an architect last year to design and build a house for me. I closed up my home in Denver and thought to hide here. It was never my intention to marry, so when he showed me his blueprint, it didn't make any difference to me what it looked like. I told him to do what he wanted, design as he saw fit because I was never sure I intended to live there, but to put in everything he would ever want in a house."

"You built a house to stand vacant?"

He smiled. "I built myself a flat-board log cabin over the ridge years ago that has suited my needs. I had no idea why I built a house . . . until recently when I knew there would be no life for me without you in it, and then it made perfect sense - we would need a place to live." He smiled with a twinkle of mischief.

"I've been at the house the past few days making sure everything was complete, but I haven't purchased much furniture for it – only for one of the bedrooms so we'd have a place to sleep, a couch in front of the fireplace, and a table in the kitchen. I thought you might enjoy making it *your* home."

Her arms were tight around his waist. "I will enjoy making it *our* home. It doesn't matter what it looks like, I just want to be there with you."

It was therefore stunning when they came over the ridge and Edward's house came into view, the only house on the hillside. He was leading the horse, they were holding hands, and he slowed for her to have a moment to absorb what he'd been telling her. There was intricate fretwork and gables, a turret, and smoke coming from the chimney.

Jordan gasped. "You said you built a house, not a mansion!" she said with awe.

"If you don't like it we can find something else. And we've never talked about it, but if you'd prefer to live in Denver, we can do that too."

"Edward, what a strange combination you are. How could I not *like* it?" she asked, holding up her skirt, hurrying up the hill to get a look at where they would be sharing their lives. Edward tied the horse to the post and stood next to his wife, gathering her in his arms.

"I told them not to paint it until you had a chance to pick the colors you wanted, so it's just a base coat."

He leaned and picked her up. "Welcome home, Mrs. Stratton." He spoke in a voice rippling with a seductive quality, carrying her over the threshold.

Her arms were around his neck and her lips found their way there. "I can't believe this is real, that we get to be together, that you don't have to go home and I don't have to lie awake at night wishing I was in your arms."

"Never again," he said, sliding her down his body, capturing her lips on the way.

"Do we have to wait for nighttime?"

"Do you want to see the house first?"

"We can wander at leisure at any time and make it our own, but I can't breathe for wanting you, so house later, please."

He groaned into her mouth as his tongue warmed her to her soul. He'd lit a fire earlier, and set more logs on the burning embers. Her eyes sparkled with a million tiny reflected flames. "My desire is to make love to you in every room, but for now, I want your first time to be in a bed as I give you a small taste of what awaits us."

The mahogany staircase fanned from the parlor on the main floor and curved on both sides again at the top of the stairs. He led her to the room just to the left on the second floor with an imposing fireplace and a brass-and-cut-crystal chandelier. She was delighted at the carved headboard, dresser, and nightstands. She caught their reflection in the mirror as she fought tears. "Don't you like it, love?"

"Edward, my heart's going to erupt with all the love I'm asking it to hold. That you thought of this, that you started this home for us before you knew there was an 'us,' it's a lot to take in."

"But you haven't even seen the true pleasure part yet," he teased, opening a door to what she thought would be a closet, but was, in fact, a wood-adorned washroom that included an elegant porcelain bathtub, a shower, sink, and indoor toilet. Jordan started laughing.

"What's so funny?"

"My father had bathrooms put in his home a few years ago, thought to be some of the finest in Denver. He's going to be *so* jealous when he sees *this*. Oh, Edward, how does it work?"

"I'll show you, then you may soak at your leisure. There are two pipes that bring water to the tub, one of which spirals through the fireplace and is heated, so you have hot water at the faucet that can be adjusted to your desired temperature. There are four such bathrooms in the home. Would you like to see them?"

"Later," she said, "there are a lot of lessons we'll learn together . . . later. Your wanton wife wants to share more than your name."

Her nerve endings tingled as he drew her closer.

"May I ask you something?" she asked. His caress stirred her hidden pulses.

"We have no secrets from each other, remember? What is it you wish to know?" His lips found their way to the sensitive hollow of her neck.

She couldn't think when the muscles of her abdomen closed like tightening coils. "Edward," she said, burying her fingers in his hair.

"Yes, love?" His tongue pressed against the pulse beating in her throat.

"Have you had a lot of experience doing this?" Her head was back, her hair cascading over his hand.

*H*e hesitated, wondering what she was really asking, considering how he should respond. "I've known many women in my life." He paused in his exploration of her ripe and luscious body that was full of promise. "None more than once, and not one I cared about as anything other than a means to an end."

He waited, wondering how she would react to his admission. When her hands started to caress his forearms in a sensual rhythm, she said softly, "Good." She saw the look in his roguish eyes and colored with pleasure, making her eager, almost greedy. "I'd hate to think neither of us knew what we were doing."

His laughter filled her. "Trust me, love. Before the night is through, we will have taught each other many things." His smile accentuated his ruggedly handsome face as he pulled the silken tie from her gown and let it fall to the floor.

She wanted him to see her, and didn't raise her hands to cover her nakedness. Her breath quickened as she watched the firelight play against his entrancing face while he stood motionless. She took a step forward, running a hand up his chest, stopping as her palm covered his hardened nipple. She closed it between her thumb and finger, causing a groan to pass his lips.

He was smooth skin and hard muscle. A slick heat formed between her legs as she thought of their day in the meadow. "May I see you as well?" she asked, reaching for his belt.

He hesitated, wrapping her wrist with his faltering fingers. She was perfection, and her flawless skin spoke to him, offering him riches he'd never possessed. She smelled of vanilla and musk, and he wondered how he would be able to touch her without finding fulfillment too quickly.

Their eyes held each other as his hand fell to his side and he allowed her to undo his buckle, then slide his pants from his hips. He stepped out of them, and she leaned to pick them up, taking a minute to calm herself as she laid them neatly across a chair and pulled the covers back on the bed. "Do you mind if I look at you?" she asked, longing in her voice as her hand found its way back to his chest.

"God, Jordan, it was my intention to take you slowly and gently this day, but you are the most glorious being I've seen. I am afraid to touch you for fear I will not be able to hold back."

The wispy fingers of desire wove down her spine and softened the flesh that would soon welcome him. Her knees weakened as she looked down his body at the magnificence of his erection. "And we will fit?" she asked, looking quickly to his face.

His tender smile assured her as he touched her cheek, ran his fingers through her hair. "It will not only fit, it will bring you great pleasure." He was barely able to speak.

"For now it is my turn," she said, her eyes again wrapping his erection in desire. Her finger whispered softly down his hard arm as he strained not to draw her to himself. She circled him, running her hand, her hands, over the rippled muscles of his back and gently cupped his buttocks.

"I have never known a woman's touch to be torturous," he groaned.

"Have I hurt you?" She didn't seem to care, continuing the gentle then hard touch she spread over him in obvious enjoyment.

"The only hurt I'm suffering is that I'm not buried deep within you right now."

The heat from the fire had warmed his back, and she ran her tongue down the center, just past his waist. She felt his muscles tighten, and wondered at the intensity of emotion her entire body felt.

"I hope you don't think me less than a lady," she said, barely above a whisper, "but I must admit, I'm feeling deliciously wicked right now." She felt his roll of laughter, but there was something different about it. This time his entire body stiffened, his hands forming fists at his side.

As she returned to his front, she could see a drop of moisture glistening on his hardened tip. His eyes followed her as her hand reached for him. "I'm not sure how long I can stand," he said, "so look your fill so we may partake of the other's pleasure."

Her finger touched the fluid and gently spread it across the throbbing head. "*Stop!* I can't take much more." When she suckled her finger and tasted his saltiness, it was his undoing. "You are beyond temptation."

White-hot heat enveloped him as he took her roughly in his arms. Her tongue rose to meet his as they dueled for satisfaction. He lifted her and set her in the center of their marital bed, settling between her legs.

She lifted to meet him, her eyes closing, her head falling back.

"Look at me, Jordan." He teased her entrance with his fingers, feeling the moisture that gathered for him.

When she met his gaze, she appeared to be glowing from within with a flame of passion. "Must we talk?" She was breathless, taking his face in her hands. "There is something I need, and you appear to be the only one of us who understands the question *and* the answer."

He kissed her. It was not soft; it was not gentle. It was an explosion of the desire that both of them were ready to share. "I can't promise I won't hurt you, love," he said, "but I can promise the pain won't last long."

Without warning, he pushed into her, hard and fully sheathed as she lifted against him to take him deeper, making her truly his wife. Within moments, she was moving in rhythm with him, making soft noises in the back of her throat, wrapping his iron shaft in the softness of her silken folds. She held nothing back as she pushed harder against him, seeking a release she wasn't sure how to find.

His lips captured hers as he slid against her, feeling her readiness to shatter around him, knowing he would bring her to satisfaction before he found his release. She called out his name as her body spasmed, tightening and clinging, bringing him to an explosion of fireworks that burned him to his depth.

As their bodies began to unwind in the aftermath of pleasure, he looked into the face of the woman he loved, and knew there was not an inch of his being that wasn't complete.

"Is it always this way, Edward?" she asked when the beat of her heart had returned to normal and she was able to form a coherent sentence.

She was cradled against his chest as he ran his fingers through her luxurious hair that at times looked the color of polished mahogany. He was glad he'd done their bathroom with that particular wood.

"Did you enjoy kissing your suitors?"

"You know I didn't," she responded.

"Sex is much the same." His lips tasted the sensitive swell of her breast. "It's the feelings attached that made this shattering. Otherwise, like kissing, it's merely mechanical." Brushing the hair from her forehead, he whispered, "In all of my years, even I didn't know it could be like this."

He put more wood on the fire as it quietly flickered in the darkness, then climbed back into bed and wrapped her warmly in his arms again. "I wanted to teach you, but you taught me more than I thought possible." His final thought before sleep pulled him into its unconscious arms was that he would have traded all of his wealth to have this woman who slept soundlessly against him.

"WAKE UP, SLEEPYHEAD," SHE SAID. "COME SHOW ME OUR new home."

He rolled over with a salacious grin. "I would've been looking for you long before I found you if I'd known this existed."

"You would've been robbing the cradle if you'd found me too much earlier, but we can take the rest of our years and perfect it. Show me how the shower works." She was unreservedly naked on the edge of their bed.

He reached over and touched one of her tempting breasts and felt the nipple harden under his thumb. "You sure you want to get up?"

"I see you've gotten up rather nicely," she teased. "But I want to try the bath." She pulled him by the hand.

"How could I be so completely satisfied, yet wake after a passionate night and want you all over again?" He followed her to their bathroom.

She was uninhibited as she showered while he shaved, a companionship neither expected.

"I couldn't have imagined this." She dried herself off. "I know married couples often have separate rooms, but I would never want you to leave me to sleep elsewhere."

She was pinning her hair when he put his hands on her shoulders and stared at her reflection. "Does it bother you when it's down?" he asked. "I love watching its movement."

"Then when we're home, I'll wear it down. Truthfully, it gets heavy when I wear it up, and I've often wanted to cut it."

He removed the pins, then lifted her, carrying her back to their bed. She was shocked at the feel of his lips on her abdomen, but began to move in abandon at the feel of his tongue, his hands.

"You steal my thoughts like aged wine," he said, continuing his caresses.

"Then we must have drunk quite a bit, because there isn't a thought in my head except the pleasure I'm feeling. What are you doing?"

"I want to show you there are many ways to make love. You will be sore from last night, but I would satisfy you in a way that will soothe you, not bring you more discomfort."

"How you might consider anything to be a discomfort is beyond me," she said with a seductive purr.

She held his hair as he moved lower, letting his warm breath meet her thigh as his lips stroked her. He wanted to savor her, and when he saw her moisture, her desire waiting to be tasted, his tongue devoured her core. Her body jerked as she cried out, bringing a smile of satisfaction and lighting the fire of his desire.

"I had no idea . . ." She moved against him harder, wilder, intense.

His lips were a flame heating her body to its ignition point, scorching her. She wanted only the release that was close. He didn't want to bring her too fast as he throbbed in rhythm to her movements against his teeth, nipping and licking the honey that flowed for him.

He quivered at her smell as his tongue circled her throbbing nub and her hips lifted from the bed to bring him nearer. He saw the quick hard pulse at the base of her throat. She was gloriously abandoned, and she was his.

He inserted a finger into her moist and swollen flesh as his tongue continued to press hard up and down the channel of her opening. She held the sides of his head tightly, pulling him closer as he inserted another finger. She screamed his name, pleasure racking her, spasms flowing around his eager lips and hand.

When the last of the tremors ebbed from her limp body, he slid up to cloak her in his warmth. His softened lips took hers in a shimmering kiss that had them both taking the other's face, joining together for an embrace that meshed their souls.

"I've always known what my parents share is unique," she said. "But I could never have come close to imagining this."

Their next several hours were spent wandering the house, deciding what each room should look like. She carried a journal to make notes so they would remember when the time came to order furniture.

She stopped in her tracks when she saw the stained-glass window in the dining room. "Edward, it's *gorgeous.*"

"The lady has excellent taste. Fact of the matter is, it's an original Tiffany, made by Louis Tiffany himself, as the hash marks on each piece indicate. That window, my darling, cost more than the house itself."

"You can't be serious?"

"Quite serious. When I gave the architect free rein, he took me seriously." He smiled. "But Louis is a friend, the window is stunning, and I have no problem whatsoever with the cost of it. I'm glad it brings you pleasure."

"It's remarkable." There was awe in her voice. "There's so much to do. We'll have such fun christening each room," she said brazenly, taking his hand. "What's next?"

The room next to the staircase on the main floor had floor-to-ceiling bookshelves. "It's so *grand*." She ran her hand over the polished oak of the empty shelves.

"Then you should appreciate opening the crates." He pointed to the far corner. When she lifted the lid of the first, she was overcome with pleasure to see it was filled with leather bound books of every description.

"These are all classics! I love to read!"

"There are classics in this crate, modern novels in another, horticultural and travel books in another. I tried to anticipate that you might have different preferences with the season or a mood."

She wound her eager hands around his waist. "I have a suggestion," she whispered seductively.

"When you use that tone of voice, my whole body is listening."

"You mentioned making love in every room in the house?"

"Right now?" he asked, cupping her face in his hands, running his tongue over her tantalizing lips.

"We can continue now." She unbuttoned his shirt and ran her tongue over his taut nipple. "I want to see you in every room, feel your love in every room, know that no matter where I am in this house, you're there with me."

"And when we've finished, we'll start again. It will be my pleasure to please you."

"Edward?" she asked shyly.

"Are you blushing?"

She nodded as she lowered her head so he couldn't see her embarrassment. "You know how you pleased me this morning?"

"You thought I might forget?" He ran his hand down the front of her gown and cradled her gently.

Her knees weakened. She had his shirt unbuttoned and was working on the fastening of his pants. "Is it possible for me to pleasure you in the same manner?"

"Oh, God, Jordan, I had no idea a woman could be so sensual. How was I this lucky to find you? You're a gem beyond measure. We'll learn many ways to please each other." He was trying to hold back his desire, but she was having none of it. She tasted the droplet that rose for her, the very texture of his soul.

He had unleashed a wanton and couldn't have been more thrilled.

When he was spent, she led him through the door that opened to a wrap-around porch. They stood arm-in-arm looking at the houses and shacks littering the far country-side. Some were barely lean-tos, others were substantial, all were either wood or painted white, but none compared to their home on the hillside. "What color should we paint the outside, do you think?" she asked, holding his hand and running her other hand over the tightening muscles of his forearm.

"Whatever color would bring you pleasure. I assure you, I don't care."

"Then let's paint it yellow so no matter the weather, we'll have our own sunshine."

"Your radiant glow is enough for me," he teased, kissing her head, "but I'll make it so."

"It never occurred to me how many things were needed to make a household run, especially when you're starting from scratch," she said, hours later, slightly overwhelmed.

"Without sounding patronizing, you may purchase whatever you wish. We'll go to Denver soon so you may select furnishings. I would live in a shack, but I want to raise our children here, so make it your home."

DAILY HE GREW WEARY OF THE DARKNESS OF MIND AND soul as they worked bringing minerals from underground. He knew he would close this mine soon and felt responsible to find employment for those who had been loyal to him.

He rode into town after a long day, knowing Jordan would be visiting her aunt. He tied his horse to the post and was just outside the door of the general store when he saw her through the window. She was kneeling at eye level with a small girl in tattered clothes.

"Mama said I can have a pair of shoes when the snow falls," the young voice said wistfully.

"Will you tell your mama that these came in for someone else who never came and got them? They fit you just fine, so you may have them."

"Truly?" the little girl said with awe. "I've never had new shoes before."

"Truly," Jordan said, running her hand over the child's hair.

The youngster ran past him, skirts held high, not taking her eyes off her shoes.

"Watch where you're going!" Jordan called after her. When she saw him, her face lit with joy. "Hello!" She threw her arms around his neck. "I'm so glad to see you!"

Holding her in his arms felt like a homecoming. When he stepped back after a passionate kiss, he saw Dorothy shaking her head as she wiped the counter.

"You two, I swear. Take her home, Edward. I'm closing up."

"You don't have to ask me twice. Did you walk?"

"Yes, it was such a pleasant day."

When he picked her up and threw her over his shoulder, they could hear Dorothy laughing. "Now that you have an idea of the pleasures to be had between a man and a woman," he said, settling into his saddle and letting her slide down his front, "this might be more enjoyable for you."

She could feel his hardness between her legs. An indecent grin appeared as she moved against him. "Yes, the last time we did this, I couldn't imagine what these feelings were about." She leaned her head on his chest and ran her nails up his back.

When his hand found its way between them, she was surprised how ready she was for him. "Is it possible to make love on a horse?" she asked between breaths.

"I imagine it's possible to make love just about anywhere if you're creative enough. But we should probably get out of town before we let things get out of hand."

Chapter Five

THE ACCIDENT

*H*e was late getting home. Covered in dirt and soot, she knew something was horribly wrong. "What is it?" She set aside her quilting and rushed to his arms.

He held her as though she were a lifeline. "There was an accident." He pulled her even tighter. "One man lost a leg, two are seriously injured."

"Are *you* all right?" She searched the face that was so dear to her.

"I was halfway down the hill when I heard the blast."

She touched his cheek. "I want to hear everything. Will you come upstairs and get cleaned up and tell me what happened?" He nodded. She led him by the hand.

She ran a hot bath as he removed his clothes. "A beam broke as the last cart of the day was being pushed out," he said, sinking into the hot water, glad that something was finally able to warm his bones. "Angus grabbed a log for support and probably saved many lives doing it. But another support broke, severing his leg."

"Oh, Edward! Will he live?"

"It will be touch and go, but the doc thinks so. We worked for hours making sure everyone was accounted for, shoring up what we could, getting help for the injured."

"Will the others be all right?" She washed the grime from his back.

"They'll live, but it will be a while before any of them can work again. I'll see that the families are well taken care of." Frustration and pain were evident as it poured from the core of his soul.

When she realized it could just as easily have been him, tears blurred her eyes. "I love your kindness, but I need you to be careful. I couldn't survive without you."

"I'll never leave you, but when issues are settled at the mine in the next few days, I need to spend some time in Denver. You'll be able to order the things you want, but we'll be there about a week. I've ordered our home to be prepared, and you should be comfortable. You'll be able to visit your relatives, although I understand your parents aren't back yet. Can you be ready?"

"Of course I can. I don't care where we are, as long as it's together." When he had dried off, she shrouded herself against his bath-warmed body. "Does Angus have a family?" She was kissing his shoulder.

"Not that anyone knows of. He's been with me a little over three years, and I've never heard him speak of anyone."

"So tragic. Promise me you won't take any chances?"

"A few months ago I wouldn't have cared what happened to me. Now, every moment away is a moment closer to being back with you." He was standing naked, his desire for her evident between them. She was fully clothed when he picked her up and carried her through the connecting door, standing her by their oversized bed.

"I know how fond you are of that particular gown," he said huskily, kissing the hollow of her collarbone. "Please allow me to remove it, or I fear it may be in tatters as I show you how thankful I am to be alive."

They lay spent in each other's arms some time later. He rubbed his thumb across her cheek, examining her face as though memorizing it. "I know we're not the first to feel such passion, but it's you and I together who create this symphony between us. It's music I will never tire of."

THEY'D BEEN IN DENVER FOR A LITTLE OVER A WEEK. ALL the necessities for their hillside home had been ordered, the fabrics chosen, and they'd spent many hours with Aunt Phoebe, who happened to have a lavish home just a few blocks from Edward's.

"I am impressed, sir," Jordan said one evening as they arrived home from Phoebe's. They were in the marble entry as he helped her remove her cape.

"Why is that?" The musky smell of her hair had him thinking lustful thoughts as he took her hand and pulled her behind him, up the winding staircase to their room.

"I was not aware you had it in you to be so socially conforming and delightful. You will surely ruin your reputation when my aunt lets it be known that you are actually quite charming."

"She reminds me so much of you, I found I could not remain stoic in her presence." He slowed as he was removing his clothes and gently pulled the pins from her hair. "Will a time ever come when I don't harden when I look at you?"

He ran a palm over her waiting breast and felt her nipple peak. "Please hasten to our bed so I may continue to broaden your education in the carnal joys of what can be shared between a man and a woman," he teased.

"There can't possibly be more, can there? In the few months we've been married, we've made love at least a hundred times. I can't imagine something new."

"Just breathing takes on a new quality when you're in my arms."

EDWARD WAS FINISHING A BUSINESS APPOINTMENT IN preparation for their return trip home tomorrow. Their Denver home on Pennsylvania Avenue boasted all of the newest gadgets and fine furnishings, but Jordan found she was excited to be returning to their honeymoon home in Nederland. She wanted to say goodbye to Aunt Phoebe and pick up a present to take to Aunt Dorothy. There was a small staff at their Denver residence, and she requested her carriage be brought around to run her few errands.

As she started to step into Edward's carriage, she heard a child's voice. "Jordan, Jordan, wait!" She hesitated. Adler was on the other side of the street running toward her. Knowing his eyes were on her and he was not paying attention, she called out to him to stop, seeing his path would take him directly in line of an oncoming trolley. He never looked, and she knew he would be trampled if he continued.

She ran with all her strength, and was thrown against the side of the horse as she reached him, turning as she fell so as to take the brunt of the impact. They were both winded as they lay there, but they didn't have the luxury of staying where they were as more trolleys, coaches, buggies, and riders covered the dusty street.

A gentleman stepped from the curb and assisted them as her driver ran to her other side. "Are you hurt, madam?"

"I don't think so. Thank you for your assistance."

She wiped dust from Adler's cheek. He seemed unphased by what had happened and turned to her with what appeared to be adoration as well as anger in his young eyes. Her body hurt from the impact and fall, and she was catching her breath when he said, "Why did you leave me?"

She was surprised at his question and wasn't exactly sure how to respond. After a moment she said, "Oh, Adler, it had nothing to do with how I felt about you. Sometimes it just doesn't work out for grownups to get married."

"My dad said you left him for another man."

Jordan controlled her outrage, trying to think of a response that wouldn't frighten the small child that stood before her, thankful her groom had gone back to their carriage. "It's true I've married someone else, but I didn't meet him until after your father and I were no longer together."

"I thought you were going to be my mom. Dad says

you're just like all the others – worthless." The innocence on his face was in such contradiction to his words. She didn't know whether to be incensed or sad.

"Take care of yourself, Adler." She crossed the street between buggies and horses and an oncoming trolley, being pushed around in a throng of bodies. The closer she got to her carriage, the more faint she felt. She swayed, and her driver took her arm.

"Are you all right, Mrs. Stratton?"

She heard him, but she was so tired all of a sudden. "I'm sorry to have inconvenienced you," she said, leaning on the rail, "but I'm afraid I'm going to have to delay our trip."

"No trouble at all, ma'am. Let me help you up the stairs."

"I'm fine, truly. Just a little shaken from my encounter with the horse."

"Shall I find a doctor for you?"

"No, no, really, I'm okay." She climbed the few stairs, wanting desperately to get inside. She had no idea what was wrong with her. She heard the butler come into the hall, concern in his voice and inquiring why she was back so soon. Jordan slipped unheeded to the floor.

When she awoke, she was in bed, Edward holding her hand, a distinguished looking gentleman on the other side. She pulled the covers under her chin.

"What's the matter?" she asked weakly. "What happened?"

"You fainted," Edward said, kissing her hand. He put his forehead into her palm. "I thought I'd lost you."

"Never," she tried to smile. "My whole body hurts." She tried to get comfortable.

"There was an accident," the kindly man with white hair said. "I'm Doctor Wheaton. I've done all I can." Looking at Edward he said, "Your husband will explain. You rest, and send someone for me if you should need anything. I'll be back tomorrow to check on you."

Edward nodded to the man as he let himself out of their room. "What is it? You have such a haunted look on your face."

"My concern is solely for you." He kissed each of her fingers and touched her cheek with compassion. "Did you know you were with child?" he asked quietly.

"What?" She leaned against the pillows, her hand clutching her abdomen. "Did I . . .?"

"I'm so sorry, Jordan."

Tears, large and profuse, flowed unheeded down her cheeks. "I had suspected, but wanted to give it more time to be sure."

His eyes closed and his heart broke, remembering walking into the house, excited to see his wife. "When I got home, you were collapsed in the foyer. I rushed to your side, having no idea about the accident you'd had. But when . . ." He took a deep breath to stem the ebony of shadows and choking the memory brought. "When I lifted you in my arms and saw you covered with blood, I knew I would die *with* you if anything happened."

"I'm sorry, Edward, so sorry."

"Hush, now." He wiped her tears. "We'll take time for you to get better, then I'll take you on a cruise. Would you like to visit Paris?"

She was surprised. "No, I just want to go home – with you. I don't need trips and luxuries, I just need you."

"When the doctor says it's okay to travel, I'll take you home, but for now you need your rest." He hesitated. "Can you tell me what happened?"

She told him the entire story, his eyes alight with something akin to fury. "Don't be angry, love, it was an accident. It wasn't Adler's fault."

"But for him to speak to you that way. He's as horrid as his father."

"He was hurt." Even in her own ears it sounded as though she was making excuses. "He thought I was going to be his mother, and I'm not sure he knew what he was saying."

"You're too good, Jordan. He was spawned from his father's loins."

They didn't speak for a few minutes, each lost in their own thoughts. "You need rest. Your body needs to heal." He thought to leave her, but she held his hand and pulled him toward her.

"Please, I don't want to be alone. Please will you hold me?"

"For as long as you need me, I won't leave your side. Rest now. You'll be sore for a while, but thankfully the doctor says you'll be all right."

She curled into his side. He held her until she was soundly asleep, but he burned with yet another reason to hate Andrew.

Chapter Six

THE PIANO

*I*t was another two weeks before he felt she was well enough to travel. Her body was healing, but the bruises were a constant reminder how close he'd come to losing her. The thought was unbearable, and he protected her like porcelain.

She was blinded by boredom.

When they'd been home for a few days, she'd had enough. "Edward, listen. You're suffocating me. I feel fine. I love how you love me, and I appreciate the fright I must have given you, but I need you to let me breathe again."

"I'm afraid to leave you alone. Every time I close my eyes, I see you spinning from the impact, I see you in a pool of blood on the floor. I see no reason to live if you're not here."

"I'm not going anywhere. It was an accident. Any more than you plan on not coming back when you leave for the mines in the morning, I'm not going to put myself in harm's way. For your sake, you need to relax. I'm too stubborn to die."

"I'll try. And when I'm not aware I'm hovering like a mother hen, remind me. I'll do my best to give you what you need."

"What I need is you, us. Fun and comfortable and sexy and living, not afraid of what might happen."

After a moment, he said quietly, "There's something I need to show you."

She was completely puzzled when he led her up the staircase, and then up the next staircase from the second floor that led to the turret. He hesitated at the door and turned toward her. Touching her face, he drew her into the room with him, closing the door behind them. It was dark, with only a few rays of sunlight filtering through the dusty window, playing with particles that hung in the air from being disturbed by their intrusion.

"What are we doing up here?" she asked, looking at the oak bookcase on the left side of the room that she didn't remember seeing before. To the right was an armoire, the same look and feel of the bookcase, and next to that, across from the bookcase, was a cushioned bench. "Are these new?"

He held her for a moment. "Jordan, there have been strange happenings recently at the mine. The foreman believes the frame in the shaft was purposefully cut."

"No! Why, Edward? Why would someone do that?"

"I'm not sure, but after your accident, which I believe was, in fact, an accident, I understood that life could be over in an instant. I will be careful, but I wanted to make sure, should something happen to me, you will be safe-guarded."

"No! Don't even talk like that! What's the matter with you?" She threw herself at him. "Please, *stop!*"

"I'm not anticipating trouble, I'm just making sure we're well protected, that you're well-protected."

"Okay, what is this about?"

He led her to the bench. "I have a friend named John. I've always appreciated the way his mind works, and when I told him what I had in mind, I left the rest to him. He took care of it while we were in Denver. I was pleased with the results."

It was Jordan's turn to laugh. "You're going to make me crazy, Edward Stratton." She looked around the room. "Is there something in the armoire?"

"Not yet. I'll leave that for you if you ever want to store anything there."

She sat demurely, hands folded in her lap, giving the illusion of calm, which she was anything but. There was a shimmer of excitement sparking between them. "God, it seems like forever," he said, tucking her hair behind an ear. "Will you let me know when you're ready again?"

"Oh, I'm ready. I've been ready."

He gave her a long, calculating look. "Are you sure?"

"Never more sure."

His mouth twisted into a seductive smile. "How did I ever live without you?" His heart was stabbed by the miracle of their love.

"Show me what we have to see before my curiosity gets the best of me, and then we'll talk about this thing growing between us." Her lips twitched with amusement as her hand found its way to his lap.

He laughed out loud.

"Oh, I've missed that sound," she said. "Now *show me!*"

"There are men who would steal what they want from anyone if they think it might benefit them. I don't plan on sharing."

"You're going to leave me in the attic?" she asked, teasing him with her primness.

"I asked John to make me a room that no one would ever find. He has accomplished that task."

Even with the mellow light of sunset streaming through the window, he picked up a candle and walked to the bookcase. "If you ever want to hide anything, feel free to come up here." He barely lifted the middle shelf and the entire bookshelf started moving, pivoting from the middle until it was perpendicular to the wall, then stopped abruptly but soundlessly. He didn't take his eyes off Jordan as it moved, and was entranced with the surprise and excitement on her face.

"Edward! That's ingenious!"

"Come and see." He held up the candle to illuminate the room within as he led her in. It was covered in dark wainscoting, and was about eight feet wide and twelve feet long.

"Can I get trapped inside?" she asked, looking from floor to ceiling and around the room reflected in the flickering light, but holding onto the wall as though she didn't trust it not to close on her.

"No, let me show you." He drew her inside, then touched an edge of the shelf and the bookcase started moving again. She trembled slightly, the candle flickering with the movement. Even with the light from the flame, it was eerily dark.

"Show me how to open it," she whispered.

"Are you afraid of the dark?" His words were tender.

"Not usually. But I must admit I have some trepidation of being trapped. I'm not sure I could go into the mines like you do each day."

He took her hand and held it toward the wall that housed the bookshelf. "You can barely feel the edge, but all you have to do is push gently on either side, and it will activate the mechanism." He placed her hand in the right spot and pressed slightly. The door opened immediately.

"I can't believe you can't hear anything when it opens."

He lowered his voice. "No one can hear you. There's no need to whisper," he teased, love shining from his eyes.

"What are we going to store in here?" she asked, looking around.

"If there's ever anything you don't want someone to find, you may put it here. But there's more," he said, hugging her. "Can you find another door in here?"

He held up the candle and shone it around the room, the fading sun peeking through the open bookcase, casting an eerie glow and moving shadows into their secluded space that would have been sinister had Edward not been with her.

She stood up straight and got closer to the wall. She walked around, nose close to the wall, fingers touching, until she was almost completely around the room. She saw a slight reflection of a long hinge and ran her finger down the edge. "What's this?"

"You're good. It took me almost half an hour to find that. Now can you figure out how to open it?" He stepped beside her to give her more light.

"Don't tell me. I want to find it myself."

After almost ten minutes, her body changed. "Found it!" she exclaimed. He delighted in her cleverness as she stuck her finger into a knothole and pulled. This time it vibrated with the friction of wood upon wood, but it came open at her urging. "What's in here?"

"Nothing except a trunk," he said, lifting the lid of the large wooden box that came almost to her waist. "However, in the room in the room in the room is a space in the trunk for something that you want truly hidden." He touched a corner of the bottom of the trunk, the false bottom springing open, again, without sound.

"Any more surprises?" she said in awe. "What's in there?"

"Deeds. If you should ever need them, there is the deed to this house, the deed to the mines, and several other deeds. You will be the only one who will know about this. It's our secret." He brushed his mouth over hers. "I want you so much."

"Then have me," she said, nails pulling along the muscles of his back.

"You sure?"

"Positive." There was a catch in her breath. "This will be our christening of the attic, although I may hold you to the fact that it's two rooms up here, so one time may not be enough."

"Once will be enough for tonight. I want to be gentle. It will be like the first time."

And it was like the first time. All of his tame intentions went out the window as his lover ignited against him, not allowing him to be soft.

"We can be moderate some other time. It's been too long. Tonight I need you as a parched man needs water. You're my oasis. I need you to slake my thirst."

He set the candle down and quenched that which drove them both. It was a long time before either was able to leave the security of their secret room to make it to their bed.

DAYS TURNED TO WEEKS AS THEY SETTLED INTO THE routine of mountain life on the edge of a tiny town. Miners' families and a small tribe of Indians worked side by side, each using the land for their own purposes. Jordan visited Dorothy often, but lived for the time when Edward came home each day. No matter how tired, no matter what troubles he faced, Jordan became the center of his universe the minute he stepped through the doors.

"Do you have a knife?" he asked one day as they sat in front of a fire that snapped and popped, flinging sparks in the brick enclosure.

"No, it would be unladylike to carry one in Denver, and I've been with you since I got to Nederland."

He reached behind him into the cushion of the couch and pulled out a long box. "Then I've been remiss in your training," he said, kissing her nose as he handed her the box.

"What's this?"

"Open it and find out."

There was a small leather case with ties around the top and the bottom. "That's so you can wear it against your thigh or your calf, whichever is more comfortable. I'll teach you how to get to it quickly." His grin was villainous.

"I'm sure you've had a lot of experience with such escapades." She frowned. "What happened before we met is of no consequence. But I fear I might use this on an unsuspecting female were she to touch you in an inappropriate way." Her tone was quite pleasant.

"Then it's good we'll never have to find out. Now pull it out of its sheath, I want you to see it."

The handle was inset with a sapphire the size of her small fingernail and surrounded by mother-of-pearl inlay. "It's exquisite," she said in awe.

"I found a stone the exact color of your eyes and had the knife crafted to fit the size of your hand. I'll take pleasure in teaching you to be proficient."

She turned it over. "It's stunning. Thank you." Almost shyly, she leaned to kiss his inviting lips.

"You make me want you even when I've just had you. Now press the button," he growled.

The shiny, finely honed blade popped open. "Oh!" she said with delightful surprise. "That reminds me of you."

"How is it we ever get anything done? We walk by each other and it's like a small explosion."

"But always delightful," she said.

"Tomorrow I'll show you how to use your new knife. Tonight I will allow you to show me your appreciation." He picked her up and carried her upstairs.

THEY PRACTICED WITH THE KNIFE SEVERAL TIMES EACH week, and when Edward wasn't home, she practiced until she was tired. She wanted to make him proud. One afternoon she saw Edward coming up the hill and rushed to prepare for his arrival. She threw herself into his arms as he stepped inside, the mellow autumn sunshine lingering warmly on their embrace.

"To what do I owe this effusive welcome?" he asked.

"I'm just glad to see you. I've been lonely today, but I've been training with the knife. I would love for you to watch and show me what I'm doing wrong. I can hit a target within inches, but the inches are what bother me. I want to be perfect."

"You are undeniably perfect." He opened the front door, looked out, then closed it and walked through the house with her. "I have a few minutes, show me what you're doing and I'll see if I can figure out where the problem lies."

After ten minutes or so, he had shown her how to correct the movement of her wrist. Time and time again she made the correction and hit the target on the bullseye. "Thank you! That's so much easier."

"You have a good eye, and I want you to learn to trust your instincts."

"What do you mean?"

"What you believe at first sight is almost always right. Your gut knows what your mind sometimes takes seconds, minutes, hours, years to figure out. If you ever feel threatened, believe that you are and ask questions later."

"That makes perfect sense. Just think of what it was

like when you walked into Dorothy's store. There was no question you were mine from that point forward. If you'd asked me that day, I probably would have said 'yes' to a proposal of marriage, that's how sure my gut was."

"Rest assured I wouldn't have asked you that day," he said, grinning as he drew her close.

She tried to pull away, feigning insult. "I beg your pardon?"

"No, I ran like a house on fire, knowing I was going to be burned. It took me at least a week to figure out I couldn't go a day without seeing you, no matter how hard I tried."

"Okay, you're forgiven – almost. Kiss me and make the pain of your rejection go away."

"I can be talked into that," he whispered as his lips found hers. As the tension built between them, he suddenly pulled away, taking her by the hand and heading toward the back door. "You make me forget my own name. Come on, I have something for you. We'll work on teaching you to protect yourself later. For now, I'm pleased you're comfortable with how to retrieve and use your knife."

"I've enjoyed it. Let's eat, master of my heart, and you can give me whatever it is when you're sated."

"Let's hold off for a minute. I'm afraid we're going to have to deal with this surprise sooner rather than later."

"What have you done *now*?"

There was a knock on the door as they came in, and Edward pulled her along to the front of the house. "Delivery, sir," the gentleman said with a slight smile. There were six men behind him who were unstrapping a large crate from their wagon.

"Excellent. You made good time. Bring it into this room, if you please," he said, stepping back to invite the man in. Jordan knew she would find out in due time what it was, but she felt like a child on Christmas morning. When they had the huge wooden box in the room, two of the workmen were taking the claw of their hammers, pulling the boards open to reveal one of the most imposing pianos Jordan had ever seen.

"Oh, Edward! It's incredible!" She was clasping her hands, trying to maintain some dignity by not actually jumping up and down. "How did you *know*?" she asked as another workman brought in the matching bench.

Edward would spend the rest of his life buying her presents to see this look of delight on her face. "Dorothy told me how much you love to play and that you have the voice of an angel. I selfishly want to benefit from your talents, and it will bring even more joy to this house."

The men removed the debris, and by the time they were gone, sweet melodies filled the air. "Dorothy didn't explain even half of it," he said as she finished her first song.

"You'd say that even if I was off key. Tell me what it is. I've never seen anything like it."

"An 1890 Conover Giraffe. There are only a few in the United States, most still being in England. It's taken almost a month to have it brought to Denver, and then several more days to bring it up the hill."

"Look at the detail!" She ran her hand lovingly across the top.

"I've become partial to mahogany." He kissed her hair, "and it has burled wood inlay. I'm glad you like it."

She threw her arms around his neck and planted kisses over his face. "You're going to get so tired of hearing me play. It's truly a passion."

"You seem to be filled with them."

She drew away and saw the receipt Edward had signed for delivery. "*Edward!*" she said, picking it up and shaking it. "Why did you *do* this?"

"Because it pleases me to please you."

"Do you see how much this cost? I could have done with a simple piano, but you had to purchase an upright grand? You did *not* need to spend that much money!"

"Eight hundred dollars was a pittance to pay to see the smile it brought you. I would gladly spend that each day to bring you such joy."

"You're hopeless." She tried to be angry, but couldn't muster any degree of upset. "I love it. Thank you." She rested her head on his chest. "When you tire of hearing my fingers on the ivories, let me know."

"Never. You will play until we are old and grey. I will hold our grandchildren on my knee while my beautiful wife lulls them with her melodious lullabies." He kissed the palm of her hand, sending shivers to her core.

"If we have several lifetimes together, it won't be enough for me to show you what you mean to me." The tip of his tongue caressed her sensitive wrist.

"Am *I* playing or are *we*?"

"You tempt me in so many ways. For now I want to sit by the fire and let you fill the house with intoxicating music so that when you're not playing, I will still hear it."

Chapter Seven

THE ANNIVERSARY

Furniture was delivered over many months, and Jordan found satisfaction in making them a home in this hillside community where Edward was gone long hours and returned wearied. Her goal was to bring peace to his life because she understood the compassionate nature hidden under his tough exterior. In any way she could, she wanted to show him how much he meant to her.

He sat in the parlor one evening trying to find a solution to an issue plaguing the mine. He saw her reflection in the dining room mirror, the firelight flickering behind her as she lit the candles on the table. He didn't think he'd ever look at her without his blood rushing, without feeling the desire only she could elicit.

"What has you so worried, my love?" she asked, speaking to his reflected image as she blew out the match. "Come sit and tell me what's troubling you."

He pulled out her chair then sat next to her. "It hasn't been that long ago I was cooking my meals over a campfire, at times lying on rocky ground, never imagining I could enjoy living in this grand house with so grand a wife."

She laughed. "Grand indeed. You know me." She imitated a dour face, raising her teacup with a pinky pointing in the air. "I'm the height of grandeur."

"You are the grandest human I've ever known. I've met a president, generals, railroad owners, multi-millionaires, and no one holds a candle to my Jordan. I wouldn't trust one of them the way I trust you."

She lowered her head and blushed at his praise. He lifted her chin with a solicitous touch. "I sense a sadness in you. Are you unhappy over something?"

"How could I be unhappy? No, but I sometimes grieve because I've been unable to give you children since . . . since the accident."

"Listen to me, love. If I never saw another person but you, I would live my life content. But for this, the only solution is to continue to practice. We did it once, we can do it again. Have no fear." He brushed his thumb across her lower lip. "Delectable," he whispered as his tongue traced the route his thumb had traveled.

"Not so fast." She served his plate, then sat down again. "Tell me what had you frowning when you were in the parlor."

"Nothing too untoward. Strange things continue to happen at the mine, and they're escalating. I'm concerned someone else will be hurt."

"Do you have any idea who's doing it?"

"None. We haven't found evidence yet of how they're getting in."

"What kind of things?"

"For instance, we recently hauled a shipment from the mine to the Assayer's office. There were six men riding shotgun with hundreds of thousands of dollars of minerals in the bed of the wagon and the fastest team of horses available. By the time the shipment arrived, there was almost fifty thousand dollars worth missing. Not one of the men saw a thing, and I'd trust every one of them with my life."

"Is it possible you have a traitor in your midst?"

"*In* our midst?" Frowning, he set down his spoon.

"I just wondered if someone could be paying off one of your men to make mischief in an effort to delay your progress."

When he didn't respond, she looked up to see him with a perplexed expression. "You're brilliant!"

"And you're just realizing this?" She feigned offense.

"Jordan, that's it! That's the missing link I couldn't put my finger on. I trust my men because most of them have been with me for a while, so I've been concentrating on someone from the outside. I've been looking in the wrong place. Thank you!"

"I'm sure you'll find whoever it is." She took another sip of the asparagus soup. "Now finish your dinner. You're going to need your strength for the, umm, games, I have planned for you later."

"Trust me, I'm ready."

"That's one of your finest qualities."

IT HAD BEEN TWO MONTHS SINCE HIS DINNER conversation with Jordan. She'd been exactly right, one of his men had been swayed by the lure of a bribe. He personally stationed himself out of sight as the shipment was readied for transport. One of his newer employees, Thornton, looked around and, believing the coast to be clear, attached a large wooden box to the undercarriage of the cart. It was clever, really. When the cart went over a bump, a plug fell out and would drop nuggets through a small opening. The box below was only so big, so there was never too much emptied. Edward watched as the cart was returned to the mine after delivery and all the hands had left for the evening. Thornton would then sneak back and remove the minerals from the false bottom.

Edward watched three shipments leave and return, all having the exact results. He wanted to see if the man was working with someone else, or if he was the sole idiot who dared to get away with robbery. After the third shipment, Edward followed him as he took a cart out of camp, the bottom of which was covered with a canvas tarpaulin. No one would think to check what he carried. Edward was not at all surprised to see Andrew was the man Thornton met.

Edward watched as Andrew and Thornton put hundreds of thousands of dollars worth of what appeared to be nothing but rock into a large drawer attached to the underside of Andrew's carriage. Andrew gave Thornton a small part of the shipment, and Thornton turned with the empty cart back in the direction from which he'd come.

As Andrew turned to mount his carriage, Edward stepped from the shadows. "Unless you want it to be your last earthly act, you'd better not take another step." Andrew turned to see Edward standing not ten feet away, gun pointed at his head.

"What do you think you're doing, Stratton? What nonsense is this?"

"You're the most brazen man it's ever been my displeasure to encounter, Harriman. But it doesn't matter. You find yourself with two choices, and neither of them will withstand an argument."

"Who do you think you are?" Andrew said with a hateful smile.

"Shut up and listen . . . closely. I'm not going to repeat myself." He pulled back the hammer on his rifle, letting the loud noise settle in as loud noises were wont to do in the quiet stillness of a peaceful afternoon.

"If my tender wife didn't have somewhat of a fond heart for the spawn you call a son, I'd kill you where you stand. As it is, she'd be upset if I came home with your blood all over my shirt."

"Why you . . ."

"*Shut up!*" Edward took a step forward, the barrel of his gun now pointed squarely between Andrew's eyes. "You're going to unhook your carriage from your horse, ride home, gather your son and your belongings, and be on the first stagecoach out of here with the break of dawn."

"You can't make me do that."

As though Andrew hadn't spoken, Edward continued. "The coach will get you to a little town in Nevada called Las Vegas Rancho. It's dusty and lonely and you're more likely to be swindled than to swindle. There you'll meet a man named Jules Everly. He works for me. For at least the next year, you will do whatever he tells you to."

"And if I don't."

"Unhook your horse, Andrew."

"No," he said, defiantly.

Edward took one shot, blowing the hat off Andrew's head and grazing his hair. Andrew took a step back. "Unhook your horse, Andrew."

Andrew worked on the mechanism to unlatch the harness from the wagon, but turned abruptly, gun drawn, and took a shot. His gun went flying as Edward's bullet grazed his fingers, drawing blood. "The next one will be through your heart," Edward said as though they were having a pleasant conversation.

"I will have someone stationed at the depot in the morning. If you and your son aren't on the coach, I will personally hunt you down and kill you – no warning, no explanation, no hesitation. If I see you anywhere near Colorado, or hear that you've left Nevada before the end of next year, I'll find you wherever you are, and you'll never know what hit you."

"You won't get away with this."

"When Thornton tells the Sheriff what's been going on, I'm pretty sure he's not going to be as lenient as I am in letting you leave town."

"Then why are you letting me go?"

"I told you, I don't like upsetting Jordan. A trial would only get complicated and drag out for a long time. They'd either shoot you or hang you, and she'd be concerned about what that might do to Adler. If you want to live, you've got one choice. Take it or leave it. If you decide not to go, I'll make sure I have a change of clothes with me so I can put on something fresh before Jordan sees how you've stained her precious Edward's shirt. Now get out of here."

Andrew wrapped his injured hand in his kerchief, then disengaged the horse with the other hand. He stepped onto the tongue of the wagon to mount the saddleless horse, then turned toward Edward. "You're not as high and mighty as you think, Stratton."

Edward took a shot that threw dirt and rocks against the horse's legs. The horse took off in a gallop, Andrew barely able to stay astride as he disappeared in the distance. As he headed home, Edward could almost admire the fact that Andrew hadn't fallen to the ground under the circumstances.

He had a man, unobserved, waiting for them to leave, who would then take the recovered nuggets to a hiding place. He didn't want to give Thornton a chance to meet up with Andrew before morning. Thornton had no clue Edward was aware of his nefarious activities, and anything Edward had to say to the scoundrel could wait until tomorrow. Tonight, Edward had a date.

WHEN HE ARRIVED, THE DINING TABLE WAS SET, CANDLES lit, both fireplaces had a roaring fire. "Jordan? Where are you?" he called, hanging his hat at the entry.

She was standing at the top of the stairs in a golden gown that was decadently translucent from the lights that glowed behind her. "You take my breath away." He stopped on the stair below her but still looked down at her upturned face that was irradiated with the flame of her spirit.

"Just hearing you call my name does the same thing for me. Hurry and get cleaned up, dinner will be ready in half an hour."

"Yes, ma'am. At your service, ma'am. Coming right up, ma'am."

"You do it so well." She kissed him as she passed him on the stairs. "But that can wait for later. I have clean clothes set out on the bed for you, not for any reason other than convenience. Wear whatever you please, but hurry with your bath. I can't wait to see you."

She had hired Faith, one of the local ladies, to prepare and serve the meal so she and Edward could spend this special evening together. After they'd been served, Faith would leave by the back door. Jordan was in the kitchen making final preparations when she heard a knock at the front. Edward was opening it as she came into the room. A gentleman stepped through the doorway, a small case in his hand, and bowed.

"Jordan, this is Mr. Sanderlin. He's going to be our entertainment while we dine."

"I beg your pardon?"

Sanderlin set the suitcase on the table in the parlor and withdrew an elegant violin. He pulled the bow across the strings, nodded, and started playing a romantic ballad. Edward bowed to her. "May I have this dance, my love?"

He took her in his arms and began to waltz in front of the fire. He moved them from room to room – parlor, formal living room, dining room, her hair and dress shimmering in the firelight. His look was one of immense pride. "You could have had anyone in the world, but you chose me. I don't think it's possible that one man could love a woman more than I love you."

Tears glistened. "We are indeed blessed, Edward. I've thought of that moment when I first saw you standing there a hundred times. Nothing in my life has ever been the same."

Sanderlin continued to play as Faith set the food on the table. "Shall we eat?" she asked. "We can finish our dance when we're through."

"I'll be back in the morning to help you clean up," Faith offered quietly.

"Oh, I'll take care of it. I don't mind at all. Thank you for your help."

"My pleasure. I'll see you soon," Faith said with a little curtsey.

There were delightful dishes with mouth-watering aromas. Jordan and Edward sat close to each other, Sanderlin playing tunes in the other room that set the mood for their encounter. "What song is that, Mr. Sanderlin?"

"*The Romance* by Amy Beach, ma'am. It's all the rage."

"It's beautiful, thank you."

She went back to whispering with Edward. He looked into her eyes, then his eyes roamed her hair, her face, and down to her exposed cleavage. "I'm not sure how you expect me to get through dinner without ravaging you. You're truly breathtaking," he said against her lips.

He sat up and reached behind him, the enchanting music surrounding them. "Happy anniversary, my darling." He handed her a long box in forget-me-not blue with a distinctive white bow. "I have another friend named Tiffany. His name is Charles, Louis' father. He makes special items." She gasped when she opened it.

"Edward! It's dazzling! But where would I possibly wear it in our little backwater town?"

"When we go to bed tonight, I want that to be the only thing on your body besides me." His grin was devilish. "It reminded me of your eyes. I wanted you to have it."

He settled the glittering sapphire and diamond necklace around her, kissing her neck as he closed the clasp. The large tear-shaped gem hung just above the apex of her breasts. "I'm not sure I'll want you wearing that in public," he said, almost with a growl. "It's erotically suggestive and makes me want to do scandalous things to you."

"If I live to be a hundred, I can't imagine I'll grow tired of your lips, your love. You're my joy, Edward. Happy anniversary." She handed him her gift.

Their eyes met. "I expected nothing."

"Good. Then you should be pleasantly surprised."

"My God, Jordan, where did you get this? It's as handsome as any gun or holster I've seen." He removed it reverently from the packaging.

"I'm so glad you like it. When we were in Denver, I visited your gunsmith. There's suede on the back of the holster, which, if you'll notice, is the color of your hair. He took great pains to match the grip to the color of my hair. And," she said, turning it in her hand, "there's a tiny sapphire on either side." She smiled as she looked into his eyes. "I wanted you to think of me when you wrapped your fingers around it."

When he could speak again, he leaned over and touched his lips to hers. "With the exception of you, it's the nicest gift I've ever received."

He stood and pulled her up with him. They swayed to the music for several minutes. He separated from her but held onto her hand.

"Thank you, Sanderlin. That was perfect." He never took his eyes off Jordan. "You have a fine talent." Edward retrieved an envelope from the top of the piano as Sanderlin packed his case. "This will not only pay for your services, it should pay for your dinner and a night at the hotel so you don't have so far to travel. We are much obliged."

"Thank you, sir, ma'am," he said, bowing. "I wish you many more years of marital bliss."

"Are you married?" Jordan asked, her arm around Edward's waist.

"No, ma'am."

"Don't settle for less than love. Days are long and life is difficult enough. Make sure you have someone that sends you over the moon, or stay single." She hugged her husband. "Trust me, it's worth the wait."

"Yes, ma'am. Thank you both," he said, blushing. "Good night."

Chapter Eight

THE RETURN

hen he was gone, they continued to stand wrapped together in the firelight. Edward put another log on, then pushed her hair back, cradling her face in his large hands. "I have a mind to take you right here, right now. What do you think of that, wife?"

She shivered like a leaf trembling in the wind just before it releases its hold so it can fly. "I think that's a marvelous idea . . . for another time. Tonight I'm feeling naughty. I want to show you how much I love you, how much I desire you, how glad I am we're married. I want you comfortable. I intend to take my time."

They blew candles out along the way as they moved as one to their room.

He put logs on the embers in the fireplace next to their bed. As he straightened, his looked stoked what was burning inside Jordan, pleasuring her in the feeling that only his touch could satisfy. "Few people ever find what we share. Sometimes I liken it to when I hit the mother lode, but that's so trivial when I compare it to what I feel for you."

He turned her away from him and unbuttoned the buttons that started at her neck and ended below her waist. He took his time, his fingers kneading her flesh as more and more of her was exposed, followed by his lips. Like satin under his fingertips, her skin glowed as flames flicked firelight around the darkened room.

He let her gown slide to the floor, and felt her passion unfurl that she was unable to hide. She turned in his arms, running her fingers up his chest and into his hair. His whiskers, while not quite visible, were rough to the touch. She took his hands in hers and lifted them to her breasts, pressing them into her mounds until her nipples were hard and the glittering sapphire blazed at their peak.

"Hurry and take your clothes off," she said seductively, climbing on all fours onto their bed. She lowered the front half of her body so her backside faced him, enticing him to partake of her pleasures. Her moisture was visible in the firelight, and he feared he might explode with the sight of her. His wife was a shameless temptress, and he couldn't shed his clothes quickly enough.

The blood raging through his body pumped energy into his movements. He approached her awaiting invitation barely able to breath. His finger entered her, a moan escaping them both. He took his slick finger and rubbed it over her sensitive flesh as she pushed against him.

He was rock hard and took her by the hips, driving into her, pulling her back against his manhood, rocking against her, his finger moving around to massage her swollen essence. She matched his rhythm and met him thrust for thrust before she rolled away from him.

"This time it's my turn," she said in a sultry voice. "Lie down. I want to explore you."

He could smell her wantonness and his excitement flared. He took his time climbing onto the bed, laying back in a casual stance, his hands behind his head.

"You want me to think you're uninterested, but this says differently." She wrapped him in her hand, tormenting, moving up and down.

"Good God, what are you doing to me?" he growled, trying to hold on to his sanity.

"I'm learning to please you like you please me. Only I think I will receive just as much pleasure." Her tongue swirled around his moistened head. Her sigh of satisfaction had him lifting his hips for her to take in more. She gladly obliged, pulling him taut as her mouth found its way down his shaft. Her tongue circled his rim, her hand and mouth moving freely, feeling his hips clench.

"Keep your hands behind your head," she said as he reached for her. "I'm not done yet."

She rubbed her breasts over him, squeezing him between them, the cold of the blue stones in contrast to her warmth, watching him watching her. He smelled of sandalwood, and everything about him was intoxicating. She straddled him, moving up his body, her tongue dancing over his nipples as she caressed his chest with her hands and lips.

Her mouth sought his, sucking his tongue while she rubbed her moistness over his throbbing erection. He lowered his arms to grab her hips, but she stalled him. "Hands behind your head," she panted as she continued to rub against him in tortuous delight.

She sat up, her weight pressing over him, and thought it was all worth it to see the desire on his face as he watched her. She looked down and saw his virility wedged between them. She moistened her fingertip with his wetness. "I love the taste of you," she said, holding his gaze. His body arched, seeking her.

His hand followed hers as he touched the droplet that escaped between them, then he moved his finger over her lips. Her mouth sought him, sucking as their gazes held, her tongue dancing as it had on his manhood only minutes before.

Waves of pleasure washed over them as she took her hand and positioned him at her entrance. She leaned on his chest as he slammed into her, taking her breath as she took him deeper, milking him with muscles that were made to accommodate him. She closed her eyes and arched backward as his fingers found her core, making her tighten even more around him.

When she felt it begin, her thighs raised and lowered her over and around him, feeling him deep within her center. He thrust inside her until he felt the spasms, knowing she was close and knowing how perfectly they fit together, tight and wet and the very definition of erotic. As she found her release and called his name, he thrust one last time, spilling his seed, feeling life rush from his body to hers.

As her body released its tension, she collapsed on his

chest. He rolled her over in his arms, resting her on his side, protecting her in his embrace. Their lovemaking was followed by a warm and comforting silence, each overcome with the intensity of what had happened between them. Neither moved for many hours, content to their souls with the situation they found themselves in.

IT WAS ALMOST CHRISTMAS. LYING IN HIS ARMS ONE NIGHT, Jordan ran her fingers over Edward's soft hair. "Would it be appropriate for us to do something for your workmen for Christmas?"

"If you want to do something, we'll make it appropriate."

"I know a lot of them have families. I've waited on many of them in Dorothy's store. I sometimes think it's the luck of the draw that's made us wealthy. I know how hard you worked for it, but they also work hard. I'd like to do something nice for them."

"You know I would deny you nothing." He kissed the tip of her nose. "What do you have in mind?"

"I thought of giving everyone a coupon, either for a certain dollar amount for each member of their family, or maybe allowing them to pick out shoes and a winter coat for each of them. I don't want to be insulting, but I want them to know how much we appreciate their loyalty. It's not an easy job."

He held her without saying anything. She leaned up and laid her chin on his chest. "You don't like the idea?" She tried to read his expression.

"I'm trying to figure out how the heart doesn't explode when it expands like this. I think it couldn't possibly hold any more, and then it does. I'll leave you to figure out the details." Running his fingers across her cheek, he said, "I'll make sure they know it was my wife's tender spirit that thought of it. God forbid they'd think I was getting soft."

"It's not completely altruistic. It will benefit Dorothy too. She'll be ordering so much from Denver, she could close down until summer if she wanted to."

"Probably not good for the town, but maybe you'd get your wish and she could take time off. But I think it's quite doable. Let's talk with her and figure out the logistics."

They stayed quietly for a few minutes. "Thank you," Jordan said, kissing his chest, running her tongue over his tightening nipple.

"For what?" His whole body tightened as her lips moved lower.

"For opening every opportunity for me." She ran her tongue over his navel. "For bringing me life." Her teeth nipped gently at the muscle on his hip. "For loving me."

There were no more words spoken between them as they shared new discoveries, new pleasures, new beginnings.

NEW YEAR'S WAS A TIME OF PROMISE SPENT WITH JORDAN'S family in Denver. Edward had no living relatives, and it was somewhat of an adjustment to be around her parents, aunts, uncles, cousins, and extended family. As much as possible they spent time at their own home and had her family visit there. Edward had meetings daily, but they were always together nights and mornings, making plans for their future, designing their life in the framework of the number of people who depended on Edward for their livelihood.

Edward insisted on hiring staff for their home, so Jordan's time was free to become involved in charities, city events, and generally become a woman of leisure. Spring became summer, and Jordan grew restless.

"Are you enjoying being here?" she asked Edward one night after the table had been cleared and they continued to sit in front of the fire.

He studied her face. "I want to be wherever you are. If being in Denver makes you happy, then this is where I want to be."

"Does your work keep us here?"

"No," he answered frankly. "We're here because I thought it brought you pleasure to be around your family, to have involvement with other people."

Jordan let out a long sigh, then started laughing.

"What's so funny?"

"I stay because I believed you needed to be here. I grow bored with the shallowness of people, flitting from one society tea to another. Although we are together daily," she said, resting her hand on his, "I miss my husband, and I long to be back in Nederland where the people are real and hard-working."

He stared at her, intrigued by the burst of blue from her eyes as the firelight reflected in her glance. "How soon can you be ready to leave?"

She sat up straight. "What?"

"I've been miserable here but stayed because I thought this is what you wanted." Their faces were close, then Jordan moved and sat in his lap, arms around his neck.

"Promise me something?" She kissed his lips.

"You know you have only to ask."

"Promise me we'll never again not be honest with each other."

"We weren't being dishonest, we were protecting the other. I should have known better. When you're ready, we'll go."

"Thank you. Thank you. Thank you," she said, planting kisses over his face. "I'll spend the day tomorrow saying my goodbyes and letting them know your business takes us back."

"You owe them no explanation, but do what you will. I'll make arrangements to have the house readied for our arrival and we'll leave day after tomorrow."

JORDAN WAS INORDINATELY HAPPY AS THEY MADE THEIR WAY home. Edward had made the trip a few times over the winter and spring, always returning to Denver by nightfall. Their buggy would arrive later in the day with their belongings, but both Edward and Jordan chose to ride their horses, often racing, sometimes having to slow down on the rough terrain, but always enjoying the freedom of being with each other again in unrestricted surroundings.

As they crested the hill, Jordan stopped, taking in the expanse of Indians. Plumes of pearl and gray and powder blue smoke rose near a large tent around which some of the men danced. "What is it?" she asked reverently.

"It's the last day of the Sun Dance." As she looked at him for explanation, she saw his admiration for the ritual.

"Each spring the Utes have a Bear Dance, which also lasts four days. The idea is to wake the hibernating bears from their winter sleep so they will lead the men to food."

"What a fascinating custom. What's the Sun Dance for?" She loved that they were whispering, even though they were at least a mile away.

"It's a time of spiritual rejuvenation for individual men, and it reinforces the spiritual power of the community. It's an affirmation of the power of the Great Spirit to bind them together. The tradition is instrumental in the survival of their people."

Neither spoke for several minutes but watched the splendor of the ceremony from their perch. "It's dramatically intriguing, isn't it?" he asked, taking her hand.

"It's so much more powerful than the emptiness socialites engage in daily, having no purpose other than to find more pleasure."

She patted her horse's neck, cooing at him for being so good and standing so still next to Edward.

"The Ute call horses *Magic Dogs*. Not very romantic."

She squeezed his hand and a pleasant smile played on her face, but she kept her eyes focused on the tents.

"I'm not sure I've ever loved you more than I do at this moment," he said simply.

Her smile grew wide. "Then let's hurry so you can show me. There must be one room in the house we haven't christened yet." The sound of her joyful laughter surrounded him as she raced up the hill toward their home.

Chapter Nine
THE GIFT

S ummer was waning and with it came the first hint of the changing color of the leaves. Jordan loved to wander into town, often stopping to see Dorothy. Other days she travelled over the hillside or down to the meadow. Sometimes she walked, other times she rode. She listened to the stories from some of the miners' families, and quietly took their tales to her empathetic husband, who listened and made what changes he could.

They both knew the time at the mine was growing short, and Edward was making plans on transitioning many of the men and their families to other locations. As she rode slowly toward the meadow one afternoon, she saw two young Indian mother's gathering herbs. One had a child on her back, the other looked lovingly at a little girl who was obviously imitating her mother by pulling flowers.

Jordan could almost feel the softness of the doeskin dresses each of them wore, one tan, the other the color of freshly churned butter with a soothing tone of sky-blue on the shoulders. The little girl wore a similar dress, hers in a matching shade of blue. Jordan sat quietly taking in the peaceful scene. Turning to leave them to their peace, she caught a movement out of the corner of her eye.

Running quickly toward the little girl was an emaciated coyote. Jordan thought to call out, but knew there wouldn't be enough time for them to understand what was happening before the predator attacked. Taking careful aim and remembering the hundreds of times she'd practiced, she let her knife fly, hoping beyond hope she'd adjusted for its speed.

In her mind's eye, the entire scene played out in slow motion. The coyote dropped from mid-air. The sound must have alerted the mother, who grabbed her child before she ever saw where the danger was, then turned to see the animal lying dead on the ground, a knife protruding from its neck. She looked and saw Jordan astride her horse, and held her screaming child tightly against her chest.

Jordan rode quickly to their side and dismounted next to the mother, putting her horse between the child and the lifeless animal. The cries quieted at her mother's soothing coos, and Jordan started shaking with the after affect of what might have happened had she not decided to come this way today.

"My name is Willow Tree," the enchanting mother said. "You have saved my daughter's life this day. I will be forever in your debt."

"I'm just thankful I was in the right place at the right time. My name is Jordan." She leaned against her horse to quell her trembling. The other lady moved toward the dead animal and came back, having wiped the blade of the knife. It was clean when she handed it to Jordan and said, "I am Chipeta. You have saved Valley of Flowers. Her father will want to thank you."

"Having her safe is all the thanks I need. I will be eternally grateful I was here. I can only imagine, if I had a daughter, that life would be busy keeping her protected." She looked lovingly at the little girl.

Valley of Flowers was twisting her mother's ebony braids, tilting her head to look at Jordan. "I think she is curious about the color of your hair," Willow Tree said with a smile.

Jordan moved closer so she could see it. As the tiny hand reached for her unbound, cinnamon-colored hair, Jordan asked, "How old is she?"

"She is two summers now and curious about everything. Thunder Cloud thinks she is the most radiant of creatures," she said with a laugh.

"Thunder Cloud?"

"My husband." She had a slight blush. "I despaired because I gave him a daughter and not a son, but he wouldn't have it any other way. She is his joy."

"I'm sure my husband would feel the same." She ran her finger down the child's nose. "I'd better go." She mounted her horse.

"If you ever need anything," Chipeta said, "you have only to ask."

"I am most content, thank you. If *you* ever need anything, you have only to ask," Jordan said kindly. "We live in the yellow house on the side of the hill." She rode away, tears treading unheeded down her cheeks.

When she got home, Edward was in the library. When he saw her, he took her in his arms and felt her shivering. "What is it, love? What happened?"

She let him lead her to the couch in front of the fire. He wrapped her in a quilt and set her on his lap. "Talk to me. What happened?"

Her teeth chattered as she recounted her tale. "Why am I shaking like this?"

"Shock, nerves," he said. "Common after the rush of danger. I was uneasy about you today for some reason, but confident you could take care of yourself."

"Really? Thank you. I wasn't afraid, and I was glad I killed him. But I keep thinking, *What if I hadn't been there?*"

"But you *were* there, and that's as it should be. Now finish telling me the story."

After she was done and the trembling subsided, he continued to hold her quietly in his arms. He smiled when he realized she was asleep, and carried her quietly to their bed.

She didn't wake until the next morning when he kissed her goodbye. "I won't be gone long, but I want you to rest. I shouldn't be away more than a few hours."

She felt happy but lethargic and took her time bathing and getting dressed. When she came down the staircase, the front door was standing open. The sun was bright as it danced its way through the open door. Outlined against the cascading rays was an impressive warrior, legs apart, arms crossed. Jordan couldn't see his face and thought she should be afraid, although she wasn't. As she came to the bottom of the stairs, she could only assume this was Thunder Cloud.

Oh, my, he was appropriately named, she thought as she saw his expression. His look was so stern you could almost see the bolts of lightning flashing from his eyes, but she knew she was being fanciful and it was just reflected sunlight. This majestic male was no threat to her. She smiled.

He relaxed slightly and asked in a deep, baritone voice, "Are you called Jordan?"

"I am," she said. They remained motionless, observing each other. Had she lost her mind? There was a giant of a man standing in her parlor, naked except for the loincloth covering him. "And you are?" she asked, not thinking him rude at all.

He didn't answer. "You saved Valley of Flowers." He continued to stare.

"I'm thankful I was there." She ran her eyes over his chest, thinking how different his smooth, glistening skin was from Edward's, and objectively decided she much preferred the hair on her husband.

After a moment his stance relaxed and he motioned toward the dining room table. There were several items, including an ivory bow with elaborate arrows, a doeskin dress in the softest of lavender color, an exquisite ceremonial gourd made of buffalo hide and filled with crystals that illuminated when shaken, and a leather pouch tied with a cord.

He picked up the pouch and handed it to Jordan. "Willow Tree says drink this every morning and every evening until there is none left."

"What is it?" Jordan asked. The design on the bag was intriguing.

"You are to drink it," he said with no further explanation. "Come."

For such a big man, he didn't make a sound as he strode out the door, and Jordan debated whether or not to follow his command. But he was who he was, and she didn't want to be churlish. She rushed to keep up with him. There were two magnificent horses tied to the front porch rail, another grazing at the side of the house.

"Yours," he grunted, pointing to the stallion and mare that were not only breathtaking, but also spirited.

In the light of day, his gaze became more intense. Uncrossing his arms, he reached out and touched her hair. She didn't move, didn't back up. What might have been a smile lurked briefly on his lips. He gave her a slight nod, turned and whistled. Without a backward glance, horse and rider were gone, racing up the hill behind the house.

Edward found her sitting on the front stairs a while later. He dismounted and tied his horse to the rail, stepping onto the porch beside her. Touching one of the horses he said, "They're superb animals. To whom do they belong?"

Jordan looked at him and looked back at the horses. "You," she said, matter of factly. "And me." She paused. "Us."

A chuckle escaped him, then her words penetrated. "That's the finest horse flesh I've ever seen. Where did they come from?"

Her mind seemed to focus. "Thunder Cloud."

The sound of his rumbling laughter had the horses shying. "My God, Jordan, I'm not sure I could have found horses of this caliber to purchase no matter what the price. He was obviously thankful?" he teased.

"Obviously."

"I'll put them in the stable. I had thought to breed horses. These may be the beginning of the finest stock in Colorado." He went to undo the reins.

"Not so fast, mister. We're in this together, remember? I'm helping."

She took a rein in one hand and Edward's hand in the other as they led them to the back of the house.

"So it appears you've had a profitable day?" he said, teasing his wife who still seemed stunned.

"It was indeed. He brought other gifts, they're inside."

They settled the horses, and while they worked they talked about their plans, what they would do with the horses, and several times mentioned that Thunder Cloud must have truly been grateful.

Later that night as they readied for bed, Jordan sat staring at Edward's chest. "What are you looking at, love?"

"I was thinking how different your chest is from Thunder Cloud's."

He hesitated in the act of taking off his pants. "Excuse me?" he said, straightening. "Should I be jealous?"

Her eyes flew to his and she hurried to stand in front of him, running her palms up his chest, then around to his back, her cheek covering his heart. "Of course not, silly. I'd just never seen another man undressed, and he was as smooth and shiny as a polished saddle in the morning sun."

"He was undressed?" he asked, trying to see her face.

His sensitive wife must have been blushing because he could feel the heat from her cheek.

"Almost," she said, "although he did wear a loincloth."

"Well, there is that." She felt the laugh down to his belly. She stood back and ran her hands over him, letting the feel of his hair tickle her palm.

"He was an intriguing specimen, and from an objective viewpoint I could appreciate his strength. But I was aware there is no one who compares to you, no one as handsome as you, and no one, no matter how attractive, that I'd ever want to be with other than you." Emotion tugged at her. "I'm so in love with you, Edward. You're the center of my universe."

"I will never have the words to describe how I feel, but I'll spend my life trying to explain." He kissed her and lifted her to their bed. Without words he spent the next hour showing her how much she was a part of him.

FALL TURNED TO WINTER AND JORDAN HAD BECOME ADEPT at riding the horse she'd named Thunder. Although Edward had given him a formal name, Jordan called his horse Lightning, and she and Edward would ride like the wind. The snow stood a foot deep now and they were unable to go out daily, but she was content to decorate the tree she and Edward had chopped earlier in the week. It would be their third Christmas together, but it would be the first time she'd made the house warm and inviting for the holiday. The meal was planned, strings of cranberries and popcorn adorned the tree, and mistletoe hung everywhere. Not that they needed an excuse to kiss, but the joy of the season infused them as they settled in with the slow, majestic ballet of snowflakes that continued to fall.

Christmas morning dawned crystal clear with the sun reflecting off their peaceful surroundings like tiny beacons. She was excited to share her present with Edward, and rushed him through his morning routine. "Come on, come on," she said. "Just put on your robe and we'll play like an old married couple – hot chocolate, slippers, robes, sitting in front of a roaring fire. It will be fun."

The joy on her face made him want to go even slower as he took his time tying his robe and putting on his slippers. "You're doing this on purpose, aren't you?" she said, hands on her hips.

"You caught me." He wrapped her in his arms.

"And that was the greatest day of my life," she said in all seriousness.

"If I kiss you the way I want, we'll never get out of here, so move on, Missus. We have gifts to open."

They sat on the floor in front of the fireplace like children, leaning against the couch, appreciating each gift as it was opened, both of them loving the other's sentiment for the items given. Each of them had one more present to give.

"Okay, let me have yours," Jordan said, reaching to get the last one. He took her hand and set it gently back in her lap.

"Not so fast there, my spirited filly. I'm afraid mine has to be the last gift of the day. So it's my turn." Palm out, fingers wiggling, he said, "Hand it over."

She hesitated, the moment of truth arriving. It was a

tiny package, and she was hoping he'd be thrilled. But what if he wasn't? She gave it to him and closed her eyes.

"It's not like you to be timid," he said affectionately. "Are you thinking I won't love it?"

"You know me so well," she whispered. "Okay, I'll watch, go ahead and open it."

He took his time removing the tissue covering the small wooden box. He removed the lid, pulling out a pair of tiny booties. His smile was warm as he touched her face and leaned in to kiss her. "Thank you," he said quietly.

"Tell me how you feel about it. Are you happy? Excited? Wondering what we're getting ourselves into?"

"Yes," he laughed. "All of the above."

"Edward, what's the matter? You don't seem surprised."

"I'm thrilled, but I'm not surprised."

"Why not?" she asked, folding the tissue.

"Because I've known for a while now, probably even before you."

"I don't believe you. How could you possibly have known?" she asked, playfully swatting his arm.

"There's not an inch of your body I don't know intimately," he said against her neck. "I know the shape of your breast and the rosy color of your nipples. I know the curve of your belly and the contour of your face. Each of those things has changed over the last six weeks, and I kept waiting for you to realize it."

"You couldn't possibly have known that long. I only recently realized."

His smile was sensitive, his touch kind. "Believe what

you will, you will make the greatest of mothers," he said against her lips.

She finally pulled back. "Edward," she asked, wringing her hands in her lap.

"Yes, my love?"

"Will you mind ever so much if it's a girl?"

He was surprised at her question, but took her in his arms and assured her he didn't care about the gender.

"Oh, good," she said, sounding relieved, "because it *is* a girl."

He laughed and said, "I'll believe you, but why are you so sure?"

She looked down almost guiltily. "The day that Thunder Cloud brought the gifts?"

"Yes?" He lifted her chin so she was looking at him.

"Willow Tree sent me a tea," she said, blushing. "I didn't know what it was, but I was commanded to drink it by her foreboding husband. It tasted good, and I had no problem having a cup for breakfast and dinner each day."

"And?"

"And I ran into Willow Tree not too long ago. She asked me if the tea had worked yet. When she realized I didn't know what she meant, she happily explained. She said she saw how I looked at her daughter longingly, and sent me a tea to fertilize me for girls. She said they only use it when someone has gone a long time without conceiving."

It was his turn to laugh. "Then a girl it shall be."

"You don't mind?"

"Good Lord, Jordan, how could I mind? She will be the best of both of us. If she has anywhere near the joy we share, she will be the most perfect child alive. Of course I don't mind."

She tucked her head against his chest. "Edward?" she said, sheepishly.

He grinned, trying to figure out what could be coming next. "Yes, Jordan?"

"You don't mind that we're going to name her Willow, do you?"

He paused, letting the name tumble through his mind. "She will be strong and protective. No, I don't mind," he said, kissing her head. "It's a perfect name."

They sat in front of the fire for a few more minutes. "Edward?"

"More surprises?"

"No. I just wondered . . . you didn't really know I was pregnant, did you?"

"Of course not, darling. How could I have possibly known?"

"Oh, good, I didn't think so. I mean, how could *you* know if *I* didn't?"

"How indeed," he said, handing her the last present of the morning. She sat between his legs, leaning against his chest, his arms around her. She delicately removed the tissue, then removed the box. Inside the box was another box. She gently lifted the lid, expecting to find a piece of jewelry.

In it, however, was a pair of miniature ice skates. "Edward," she breathed, turning in his arms. "How am I ever going to hold all of this love?"

Kissing the tears from her cheeks, he wrapped her tenderly in his embrace. "How indeed."

BEHIND THE STORY

Growing up on shorelines, I ached for the sound of crashing waves when I went away to college in Boulder, CO. Coming around a mountain pass one day, my heart sang at the sight of a wide expanse of water, and from that moment on, Nederland became my favorite haunt.

Months later, sitting in a snowstorm in my car, watching angry whitecaps form on Barker Reservoir in Nederland, I had my first experience with thundersnow, a strange phenomenon of thunder reverberating in the confined space of heavy snow clouds. When I decided to write my first book, I used a profession I knew (Realtor), and a place I loved (Nederland), and the *Thunder on the Mountain* series was born.

In *Thunder Struck*, Book 2 of the series, Jordan and Brandan discover century-old journals as they remodel their Victorian mansion. I was so enamored of the authors of those journals and the lives they'd lived in a remote Colorado mountain town, that Jordan and her daughter Willow got their own stories. I hope you've enjoyed reading about their lives as much as I enjoyed the telling.

Honest reviews are always helpful. If you would be willing to take a moment to review Jordan's Gift (or any of Mimi Foster's other books), it would be greatly appreciated.

EXCERPT FROM WILLOW'S SECRET

Book 5 in the Thunder on the Mountain Series

Denver, Colorado
   Circa 1910

It was the third time this week the boy stood on the platform, unnoticed by those gathering in the early morning shadows, a wide-brimmed hat covering his face.

The cheerless whistle preceded the lights from a train as the mass of metal slithered over hills and around corners like a monstrous snake approaching the waiting crowd. The shrill scream of brakes broke through the rising steam from under the locomotive, adding a sinister eeriness to the dawning light of day.

Passengers disembarked, smiles and hugs were exchanged, and within minutes, only the sounds of silence with an intermittent blast of pressure from the train's engine could be heard. The young man moved from behind the pillar, head down, pulling his hands from his pockets, shoulders relaxing, and walked briskly to a waiting horse.

Appearing to have second thoughts, he retied the reins to the hitching post and took the stairs two at a time, boots echoing heavily on the boardwalk as he hurried to the telegraph office. Something about the kid had intrigued Charles, and he stepped in behind him as the juvenile approached the counter.

"Good morning, Mac. Do you have a telegram for me?" the soft, melodic voice inquired. Charles was rocked back in his boots. Was it possible the lad in Levi's and a fringed leather jacket he'd observed for days could be a girl? The wide brim still hid the face, making recognition impossible.

"I was going to send someone to the house in a while," Mac said, looking at the adolescent with compassion as he slid the envelope across the desk. "The wire's from your dad's partner. I'm real sorry."

The slight-framed urchin read the note, looked at Mac, then read it again.

"My condolences about your father's death, Miss Willow. You let me know if I can do anything for you or your Ma."

Miss Willow . . . So the young man who intrigued him was, in fact, a girl. He'd never seen her features, and they remained concealed as she peered out on the gloomy day through the paned windows covered with soot from the smoky trains.

Lowering her head to her hands, her shoulders began to shake. His eyes met Mac's in sympathy as Charles moved to rest a hand on her slender shoulder.

"I'm sorry for your loss, Miss. Is there something I can do to be of assistance?"

Barely reaching his chin, she looked up with shocking blue eyes that pierced him to his soul, taking his breath as long lashes hurriedly fanned downward to conceal apparent mirth.

"Are you all right?"

"Oh, yes. I'm wonderful." Her voice was gentle and her eyes alight, and something in his world changed irrevocably.

"I'm not sure I understand. Didn't you just receive news about your father's death?"

"Oh, he wasn't my father, he was my stepfather. In a stroke of poetic justice, he was crushed in the streets of Las Vegas by a runaway horse in exactly the same manner he had my father murdered."

Charles was considered intelligent by most standards, but his mind was having a hard time processing her words as everything about this emerging woman threw him off kilter. "Do you have anyone to help you?"

Her eyes focused on the dingy window again. "We won't need any help now that he's dead, thank you." Her voice was distant but silvery.

She engaged his eyes with her delicate smile. "This may give my mother more time, knowing she won't have to face him again."

Nodding her head in dismissal, the sound of her boots on the well-worn planks echoed in the morning stillness. "Thank you, Mac. Please send word immediately if you have any hint of his spawn returning to town." Her regal tone was in complete contradiction to her boyish appearance.

"Will do, Miss Willow." He didn't bother to hide his amusement.

Charles stood in the doorway, watching her mount the horse as though she'd been born in a saddle. Long locks of chestnut brown hair broke free of their confines with the rhythm of the horse's canter, flowing with the wind as she disappeared in the distance.

"Who is she, Mac?"

"Willow Stratton, daughter of Jordan Harriman, one of the most splendid women God ever created. You could have blown me over when she said that about Andrew. I had no idea."

"Tell me about her."

"Her Ma was pregnant with Miss Willow when news came Edward Stratton had been killed. The whole town mourned. Never saw a man adore a woman as much as he cherished his wife. Good man, kept to himself, but people thought highly of him. I never heard any hint before today that the accident that took his life might have been deliberate."

"Do you believe her?"

"Course I do. Miss Willow and Miss Jordan are the finest around. Everyone was sorely dismayed when she married the scoundrel Harriman with Edward not two months in the grave. Life musta been hard to be almost ready to have a baby and your husband gets killed. She was never the same. Not one soul around who wouldn't have looked out for her."

"When was that?"

"Happened back in the early '90s, but Miss Willow's a lot older than her years. Why you so interested, Charles?"

With a cordial tip of his hat as he walked out the door without a backward glance, he stunned the proprietor when he said, "Because when the time's right, I'm going to marry her."

AUTHOR REQUEST

In this day and age of eBooks, eReaders, Amazon, Kindle, Barnes & Noble, Goodreads, and similar venues, Reader Reviews are the lifeblood of today's authors.

If you would be willing to take just a minute before you go and leave an honest review at the vendor from whom you purchased this book, and/or on Goodreads, it would be helpful and very much appreciated.

And if you loved this story, be sure to sign up at Mimi Foster Books to find out when the next book is scheduled for publication.

CURRENT BOOKS

By Mimi Foster

THUNDER SNOW – Contemporary
Thunder on the Mountain Series Book 1 – stand alone
Jack and Callie
An admired but reclusive businessman wants nothing to do with emotional entanglements. When a self-sufficient redhead invades his sanctuary, he must set aside his past to protect her from a stalker bent on destruction.

THUNDER STRUCK – Contemporary
Thunder on the Mountain Series Book 2 – stand alone
Brandan and Jordan
*Betrayed New York lawyer escapes to an isolated town. As she and a local builder remodel a Victorian mansion, they find old journals that mirror the present as history begins repeating itself. (**MADELINE MANOR** is the "sweet" version.)*

THUNDER STORM – Contemporary
Thunder on the Mountain Series Book 3 – stand alone
Miles and Jeni

A blaze of fascination ignites each time the zany New York ad executive and a hunky Colorado contractor meet, but neither is willing to get involved in a long distance relationship.

JORDAN'S GIFT – Historical Novella
Thunder on the Mountain Series Book 4 – stand alone
Edward and Jordan
A hardened mine owner has little tolerance for people until he encounters a fiery newcomer who is running from the conventions of society and a broken engagement to his archrival. He will do anything to protect her from the smooth talking, black hearted, jilted fiancé.

WILLOW'S SECRET – Historical
Thunder on the Mountain Series Book 5 – stand alone
Charles and Willow
She's too busy for daydreams of handsome heroes, but a generous, well-respected railroad heir has no shame in fanning the fiery flames of attraction that spark every time he and the vibrant young woman are near each other.

STEALING RUNNER'S HEART - Contemporary
Leaving the Game Series Book 1 - stand alone
Runner and Charlotte Rose
When she was a child, he was her hero. When she grew up, he was her dream. When he brings home a fiancé, Charlotte is determined to carve out a new life for herself. But before the final curtain falls, is it worth one more chance to go after what she wants before her dreams are extinguished forever?

MAISY'S MIRROR – Contemporary

Non-series – stand alone
Wills and Maisy
A young widow living in seclusion buys an antique mirror and falls in love with a handsome reflection who shares an intriguing tale of love and betrayal. Will she find the strength to convey his story to release him from his ethereal prison and from her life?

I love to hear from readers, so drop me a line at mimi@mimifoster.com or follow me on my website MimiFosterBooks.com.

ABOUT THE AUTHOR

Bestselling writer of romance novels in the early morning hours, award-winning Realtor during the day, Mimi is an incurable romantic who loves to create sexy but tender escapes about unforeseen encounters that forever alter lives for the better.

In addition to being married to her perfect human, Mimi is a blogger and photographer. She made five perfect female humans (her greatest achievement). They, in turn, have made five more small perfect humans.

She loves to hear from readers, so be sure to find her on her website (MimiFosterBooks.com), or interact with her on social media.